The Mask Behind the Face

Pendragon Press

The Mask Behind the Face

Stuart Young

First Published in 2005 by
Pendragon Press
Po Box 12, Maesteg, Mid Glamorgan
South Wales, CF34 0XG, UK

Typesetting by Christopher Teague

ISBN 0 9538598 3 5

Printed & Bound in the UK by
Antony Rowe, Eastbourne

Introduction...1
The Mask Behind the Face.........3
The Death of Innocence...........52
Daddy's Little Girl......................59
Mr Nice Guy...............................62

For Ivy Hynd

Publishing History

'The Mask Behind the Face' is original to this collection.
'The Death of Innocence' was previously published in *Nasty Piece of Work #9* (1998)
'Daddy's Little Girl' was previously published in *Nasty Piece of Work #2* (1997)
'Mr Nice Guy' is original to this collection.

Introduction

Reading again the tales that comprise this book, Stuart Young's second print collection of short stories, I am reminded of how the author's central concern in his work is human vulnerability. In fact, I think I would be hard-pressed to identify a truly monstrous character appearing anywhere in what fiction by Young I have read. To those who favour humanism this is doubtless much to his credit since, however difficult it may be to accept the fact, those whom we believe to be our enemies are often acting in pursuit of what they hold to be a greater good. Young can take us inside the minds of characters that we may find initially repellent and force us to see the world through their eyes. Some years ago he caused a furore in the small press with a story about a Neo-Nazi, and how this individual justified his actions. It was a brave story, because I know that Young disagreed vehemently with every word he penned in the tale in defence of the character.

But if Young is thoroughly attuned to the nuances of character and holds the view that wickedness is in the eye of the beholder, this does not lead him as a writer into the morass of moral relativism. That trait I have already mentioned above, human vulnerability is also evident in another of Young's literary concerns. In story after story one cannot fail to notice a common thread, or pattern in the carpet, and this theme is the loss of innocence. The three stories included in the present volume alongside the title novella are all concerned with naivety undone by the harsh realities at the cutting edge of experience. Young shows us that a pure heart is just as likely to become corrupt or be consumed by corruption as is any other. The story "Daddy's Little Girl" is particularly chilling in this regard. It is never made entirely clear whether the horror waiting in store for the child relating the tale is real, or whether the horror is mostly in a warped taken-for-granted expectation on the part of the reader.

One other aspect of Young's work deserves consideration here, bound up as it is with the loss of innocence and vulnerability. There is almost always present in the stories some depiction of masculinity in crisis. Many of Young's male characters are tormented by self-doubt and seem constantly on the verge of the "fight or flight" impulse. Young's female characters are often self-assured and worldly-wise in a way that his male characters are not. Moreover, there are none of the dubious femme fatales common to weird fiction in Young's work and where patriarchy is present it is a concept shown as being riddled with intrinsic flaws.

The merits of these short stories aside, the title novella is undoubtedly the most impressive piece of fiction in the present volume. It shows a grasp of the scope and complexities of religious and metaphysical tenets that is rarely achieved in weird fiction. I was not previously aware of the existence of Pick's Disease and the skill Young displays in fusing this obscure malady with a debased Gnosticism is nothing short of breathtaking in its originality. In this brilliant novella Young really cuts loose, positing a series of insights that transcend the questions we as human beings inevitably ask when confronted by the tormenting concepts of infinity and eternity. Young has his central character Craig utilise the eastern Mandala in his quest for meaning. But that mystical and personal glyph, which prompted C.G. Jung to claim it was the ultimate key to the self, is finally revealed as only another mask (c.f. the Buddhist concept of "Maya"; the world as illusion). This shows a sardonic aspect in Young's writing that reminds me of the lines from Lord Dunsany's classic tale "The Hashish Man":

"Once I found out the secret of the universe. I have forgotten what it was, but I know that the Creator does not take Creation seriously, for I remember that He sat in Space with all His work in front of Him and laughed."

Stuart Young shows us a Creator who is not laughing. You'll have to find out for yourself what He is actually doing in the pages that follow. Along the way you'll even take a look through His eyes. You will not be disappointed.

Mark Samuels
London, England

Mark Samuels is the author of the BFS award-nominated collection *The White Hands and Other Weird Tales* published by Tartarus Press, and *Black Altars* from Rainfall Books. His next volume, a novella called *The Face of Twilight*, will appear under the PS Publishing imprint in late 2005.

The Mask Behind the Face

"The master of the monstrous… the discoverer of the unconscious."
Carl Gustav Jung on Hieronymous Bosch

My thoughts shine like stars.

And like stars they fade in the face of the coming dawn. Bright points of luminescence; dulling, dwindling away to nothingness.

The stars know they will return the following night. But I'm not so certain about my thoughts' fate.

What will the morning bring for me?

*

I hate mornings.

Dragged from the safe cocoon of a warm bed, the worries and concerns of the outside world forcing themselves upon me, assaulting my sleep-addled brain with sensory overload; curtains swishing open, birds twittering, sunlight beaming into my sleep-encrusted eyes. This is my idea of Hell.

It doesn't help that Paula's a morning person. "Up you get. Don't want to be late for church."

Church. It's Sunday. God, this gets worse.

The shower wakes me up a little, not much. The coffee does a better job but despite a valiant effort it's still fighting a losing battle. So much so that Paula drives us to the church in her car. My car stays in the drive. There are other reasons for her driving of course but I'm too tired to argue the point.

Sophie sits in the back seat, playing with her Barbie. "Mummy, can I go play round Debbie's after church?"

3

Paula tilts her long Audrey Hepburn neck to look at Sophie in the rear-view mirror. "Only if it's okay with Debbie's mummy, sweetheart."

I stare at the creases around Paula's neck. She never used to have those, surely she's too young to have them now, she's only thirty-four. But there they sit, marking her age like the rings on a tree trunk.

She catches my gaze. "What are you looking at?"

"Your neck."

On our first date I told her that her neck was the first thing I noticed about her. She had been poking her head around a door at the bank where she used to work. I stopped and stared; her neck was so graceful, twisting round the door like a ballet dancer. I was smitten. And when I saw the rest of her I was even more impressed.

The thirty-four year old, creased neck Paula smiles, no doubt thinking I'm being romantic.

*

The vicar's sermon drones on.

Something about love thy neighbour or the Lord will smite you. Probably. I stopped listening ten minutes ago.

Beside me Sophie squirms on the pew. She wants the sermon to be over so she can meet up with her friends in the Sunday school. Where Bible stories are told as high adventure and the kids get to draw pictures or make collages of the most exciting scenes.

But for now she's trapped here. Just like the rest of us.

Glancing at Paula I see she's rapt by Reverend Palmer's performance. Her blonde chignon nods in agreement whenever he says anything especially profound. Other people in the congregation also seem to think this is the greatest piece of oration since Moses came down from Mount Sinai. Curious, I search for another bored face.

Kids don't count. Kids are always bored unless they're allowed to run around or make lots of noise. Preferably both. But there's got to be another adult who's as fed up as I am, who feels that their life is being sucked from their body by each new word Reverend Palmer utters.

Yet everybody seems perfectly happy. The only discomfort that passes over their faces is when they notice me looking at them. Everybody knows about my problem, they all pray for me daily. But that doesn't mean they know how to respond when they actually have to interact with me.

The figure of Jesus on the stained glass window at the rear of the church draws my gaze. It's the crucifixion, reworked in jagged crystalline form, all sharp edges and bright colours. The halo shining about his head, his arms outstretched in agony, his face a mask of beatific despair.

4

Finally, someone who looks as tormented as I am by Reverend Palmer's eternal droning.

"And so God watches over us," says the vicar. "He is ever-loving, ever compassionate —"

"Jesus fucking Christ," I shout. "Why don't you just shut up?"

*

The drive home passes in silence.

Paula's embarrassed that we were asked to leave the church but it meant missing the end of the service so I'm not complaining. I still love God I just hate sitting through Reverend Palmer's sermons.

As soon as we get home Paula sends Sophie over to play at Debbie's house. Then she potters about the kitchen, trying to avoid me. A frost hangs in the air about her but she won't tell me what it is that I've done wrong.

That's how the doctors told her to deal with my condition. Ignore any disruptive behaviour, only respond to the positive stuff.

I have Pick's disease. My neurones contain tangles of tau protein called Pick's bodies which are causing my frontal and temporal lobes to atrophy. As one part of my brain dies another portion takes over, giving me new attitudes and behaviours. Lack of social skills, changes in sexual attitudes, changes in my sense of humour, obsession with certain types of food. All these things are happening to me.

At least that's what people tell me. I don't feel any different. As far as I'm concerned I'm acting exactly the same as I've always behaved. I only have other people's word for it that I've changed. This could all be some elaborate hoax.

Paula pulls carrots and potatoes from the kitchen cupboards. "I'm going to start the dinner. You go have a rest."

The aroma of roast beef wafts up from the oven where she set it on a low heat before we headed off to church. But that's not what I want. "Have you got my tortillas?"

Paula points a weary finger to the tortillas on the sideboard. I brighten. "Great. I'll put a video on."

I hear the scraping sound of Paula peeling the potatoes as I run my fingers over the cases in the video collection. I choose the 1978 version of *Invasion of the Bodysnatchers* that I taped off the telly the other week. The idea of watching a film where people awake to find themselves with altered personalities that disturb their loved ones seems ghoulishly appropriate.

Flopping down on the sofa I thumb the remote. Lines of fuzzy static flicker across the screen then the picture clears and Paula and a group of

5

her friends appear on the screen. I recognise it as a party from five years ago. Someone's obviously put an old home video in the wrong case.

Or maybe I taped over the home video by mistake. I watch the replay of the party, waiting for it to be replaced by the film.

A man slumps onto the sofa beside Paula. I recognise his face but not his manner. He's too eager to let others have their say even when they're talking rubbish, too quick to laugh at other people's feeble jokes. The man's clearly an imbecile.

It's me.

Above the babble of voices and the background music – The Prodigy playing 'Out of Space' – I hear someone ask the old me a question.

"What I never understood about religion is that you've got God, right? And you've got Jesus and the Holy Spirit. And they're all supposed to be the same person?"

"That's right," replies the stupid me from five years ago.

"So, what, God's got Multiple Personality Disorder or something?"

Instead of punching the stupid twat in the face the old me just smiles politely.

"Mind you, that would explain why God's such a contrary bastard. All that smiting and stuff in the Old Testament and then all hippyish in the New Testament. Depends what personality's running the show that day."

I stab the off button, zapping the annoying git out of existence. I wish I could've done that to him five years ago.

*

"I really think it's what you need."

Paula and I exchange dubious glances. Zoë's a good friend but some of her ideas are a little off the wall.

She sits on the sofa in our lounge her legs not so much crossed as plaited, one leg wrapped around the other like a pair of mating snakes, her face lit up in her best mega-watt smile. "I've been going to this meditation class for months. I feel so much better. You will too."

I pinch the bridge of my nose between thumb and forefinger. "Zoë, I have Pick's Disease. That's not going to be fixed by me sitting in the lotus position and going 'om.'"

Zoë pulls a face. "I know that. But the meditation will help you chill out, handle things better."

"We have the support of God and the church to help us through this," says Paula.

"Even after Craig's outburst this morning?"

"Doesn't matter," I say. "I get all the relaxation I need from my painting."

Paula gives me a funny look. She probably wanted me to focus more on the idea of the church. It doesn't help that she's jealous of Zoë. She doesn't like the idea of me being so friendly with one of my old girlfriends. Not that she'd ever admit it.

Zoë cocks her head to one side. The motion sets her earrings swinging. Large circles of thin wire, they look like they belong on a hoopla stall. "I still can't believe you've started painting. You don't have an artistic bone in your body."

"Thanks. I'm actually bloody good."

"Not judging by the pictures I've seen."

"Philistine. Anyway, that was weeks ago. The new one's much better."

Zoë looks to Paula for confirmation. Paula nods. "He's really improved. Coming on in leaps and bounds."

"This I've got to see." Zoë jumps up from the sofa. "Come on, let's go and look at your matchstick men."

As we head out to the garage where I keep my makeshift studio I study the two great loves of my life. Paula's tall and slim, bordering on skinny, her small breasts tiny bumps poking through her T-shirt. Her face looks slightly gaunt, as though her worries are weighing her down. My fault I suppose.

Zoë's slightly shorter, her brunette hair worn in a bob. Despite all the yoga she's done in recent years she's not lost her curves, just kept them nicely toned. She's always had an attractive plumpness about her – provocatively rounded is the phrase she prefers – but I'd expected it to turn to flab by the time she hit thirty. Yet here she is six years past her perceived sell-by date, proving me wrong by looking just fine.

As we enter the garage the smell of engine oil and the texture of grease greet me like old friends. But their companions, the tools, the piles of engine parts, cause me embarrassed confusion. People tell me I've been introduced to these items, worked with them for years in fact, but I cannot for the life of me remember their names. The foot long piece of metal with a hexagonal hole in one end. The thin cables with the attachments like a toy designer's idea of a shark's jaws. The long metal tube with a bulge two thirds of the way down like a python digesting its prey.

I don't recognise any of them.

It doesn't bother me though. Not now. At first, when I couldn't remember how to fix a customer's car or how to help a neighbour with an oil change, it was a problem. But that's when I thought I still knew how to be a mechanic, striding in, confident in my abilities only to discover holes in my knowledge. Holes that grew steadily bigger, becoming gaping chasms, eventually leaving nothing but an empty void. Once I reached that stage the problem ceased to exist. I handed over the repairs side of my business to my assistant Dave while Paula balances the books. It means extra work for her after she's finished her daily business as a financial advisor at the bank but that's okay, she'd tell me if she couldn't handle it.

Now I'm a househusband. I still remember how to cook and clean (although Paula's not entirely convinced on that last part) so that's what I do.

That and my painting.

Art never held any interest for me before. Unless you include my attempts to convince an old girlfriend that *Playboy* centrefolds are art. But since the Pick's Disease kicked in I've discovered a strange passion for painting.

At the far end of the garage a stack of my early efforts waits to be thrown in the rubbish. Zoë's right, they're excruciatingly bad. But next to them, beneath a sheet stained with oils and watercolours stands my current effort.

Zoë eyes the sheet, smirks. "Go on then. Amaze me."

I whip the sheet off with a flourish that would do a matador proud.

Zoë gasps.

Clouds fill the canvas. Soft wisps of airy nothingness that I've somehow managed to capture with my brush. And amongst the clouds human figures soar high above the earth. Maybe they're spirits, maybe they're angels, I don't know. All I know is I felt compelled to paint them, outlining them in gilt-edged fire as they catch the rays of the sun that shines on the right-hand side of the canvas.

Pride pulses through me. After my initial stumbling steps as a painter I've finally produced something that deserves the name art.

Zoë shakes her head, lost for words. "I don't know what to say. It's… it's awful."

I swing round, my jaw dropping and my cheeks burning.

Zoë raises her hands. "Joking! It's actually really good. God, your face when I said I didn't like it!"

Laughing, she steps forward to take a closer look. Paula touches her hand to my shoulder and smiles, amused by my fragile ego but also attempting to soothe it. Embarrassed by how strongly I reacted to Zoë's criticism a second wave of blushes hits my cheeks. I'm glad there's not a heat detector in the garage because otherwise I would have set it off by now.

Zoë leans in close to the picture, her head tracking across the canvas as though following a hidden thread secreted within the painting. "Seriously, Craig, this is fantastic. Did you take lessons while I was away or something?"

"No, I've been looking at some books on art, seeing which artists' work appeals to me, but I've not taken any lessons." It's a bit late to try for false modesty but I attempt it anyway. "This is just beginner's luck I suppose."

"Really? Wow." Zoë looks back at the canvas. "You know, this reminds me of Michelangelo. That one off the Sistine Chapel, *The Creation of Adam.*"

"Oh puh-lease." Paula rolls her eyes in mock despair. "Don't make his head bigger than it already is. I have to live with him you know."

"I tell you what," says Zoë. "There's something that would make your pictures even better. There's a brilliant technique we do at my meditation class where you imagine stepping into a picture and walking around inside it. Really helps your visualisation." Her face lights up and she rests her hand on my chest. "You should come along to the class and my teacher can show you how to do it."

I sigh, knowing she won't give up until she gets her own way. "You thought up that whole spiel while we were still sitting in the lounge, didn't you?"

"Of course not." She looks offended at the suggestion. "I thought it up on the drive over."

                                   *

"These people are freaks."

Paula nudges me. "Shh, they'll hear you."

"So?"

The meditation class hasn't started properly yet but that doesn't stop most of the class going through their paces on their own. Some stand on one leg, arms stretched high overhead. Some entwine their fingers in awkward contortions that look as if they will hasten the onset of arthritis. Some kneel on the floor, splayed fingers resting on their knees, tongues poking from their surprised mouths. In an ancient temple in the Far East I might accept their actions but in the middle of a sports centre it just looks silly.

"Can't we go play badminton or something instead?"

"No, we can't," says Zoë. "I already told Justin you're coming. If you don't show up it'll be embarrassing for me."

"Whereas me trying to wrap my legs around my neck will make me look dignified."

Zoë pokes her tongue out at me but not as a meditation technique. She steers Paula and I between the yoga mats over to a tall man who stands on the other side of the room. "This is Justin, my mediation teacher. Justin, this is Craig and Paula, the couple I told you about."

9

Justin extends his hand. "Hi."

He has a firm grip, not surprising as his sports vest shows off his muscles. Lean, stringy muscles, the kind that come from doing yoga and Pilates rather than pumping iron. Tattoos run up his arms and across his shoulders. Black tribal stuff, Maori I think. Very trendy. He needs the muscles and tattoos because frankly he looks kind of nerdy. His nose is too beaky and his goatee can't disguise a weak chin. And there's something else – it takes me a second to realise what it is – he's wearing glasses, the rimless kind that seem to pop in and out of existence depending on which angle you're looking at them from.

Frowning, I point to the glasses. "You should either admit to wearing glasses and get some real frames or else wear contacts. Those things you've got on are just annoying."

There's an awkward silence.

"What?" I look at the others, confused. "What'd I say?"

Paula throws Justin an apologetic smile. "I'm sorry, Craig's got Pick's Disease. It affects his behaviour so sometimes he can be a little rude."

"I wasn't being rude. If I was being rude I'd say those Lycra shorts make him look gay."

Another silence. Paula buries her head in her hands.

"I didn't say he *was* gay. I know he's straight. Zoë was shagging him until she got bored and dumped him."

Zoë grabs my arm and propels me towards the door. "Outside. Now."

As I stumble past the meditators I try to work out why she's upset. "What're you doing? You said I'd embarrass you if I didn't do the class."

*

I rinse my brush, the water turns to swirling clouds of green. The canvas is covered with a light green wash. I don't know what the picture will be yet – a field, a rippling green ocean – but green just felt like the right colour to start with.

Very Zen. Maybe the meditation class is rubbing off on me.

After my 'outburst' Zoë had dragged me back in there. But only after establishing some very firm ground rules. Namely that I kept my mouth firmly shut. I still couldn't work out exactly what I'd done wrong but I went along with what she said.

Fortunately Justin didn't make me do any of the poses where you needed to be triple-jointed. Just some simple stretches and then some deep breathing and visualisation. I've got to admit I found it very relaxing.

Paula didn't enjoy the class so much, she felt uncomfortable about toying with Eastern philosophies. But she liked Justin. Even as she fidgeted and complained about the meditation exercises she removed her hair band and stroked her hair: her favourite mating signal. I couldn't see the attraction myself, take away the tattoos and the lovingly cultivated physique and he'd be nothing special. But then I saw it. He has this inner energy, a way of modulating his charisma to perfectly fit the person he's talking to. If a person needed relaxing he was all languid charm, his voice a soothing aural massage. If they needed energising he became all friendly enthusiasm, so sure in your abilities that you couldn't bear to let him down. It quickly became obvious that all the women in the class wanted to sleep with him. And I think at least one of the men too.

So I'm glad that Paula isn't going again. We couldn't get a babysitter for Sophie every Thursday so Paula will stay home to look after her. Justin may be a really nice person but if he ever touches my wife I *will* rip his arms off.

I step back from the canvas, contemplating what to add to the initial layer of green. An image begins to form in the back of my mind but it's faint, indistinct. Come on, concentrate. Just reach out and wipe away the haze that obscures it. Let it become clearer, clearer –

"Daddy, I can't sleep."

The image vanishes. I spin round on Sophie, seething. "Can't you see I'm busy?"

She looks so tiny in her Tweenies pyjamas, dwarfed by the engine parts and toolboxes. She stands there, clutching her Barbie to her chest.

"What do you want, Sophie? You know you're not supposed to come in here by yourself, especially at night."

She doesn't say anything, just gazes up at me as though she's not quite sure what I'm saying.

"Look, either tell me what the problem is or go back to bed."

Her lip wobbles. "But I can't sleep!"

"Well, try!"

She hesitates, shifting her weight from foot to foot. Then she speaks again, her voice quiet, subdued. "Mummy says you're changing."

Oh God. We explained about my disease before but how do you explain these things to an eight year old? I put down my paintbrush. "You already knew I was changing."

"I don't *want* you to change." Typical eight year old; sulky, demanding.

I try to remember what Paula and I said to Sophie last time we spoke about this, what new angles I can use to explain things more clearly. Sophie's usually okay with my illness, it's only when we sit her down to have heavy discussions about it that it freaks her out. "Why not?"

"You yell at me now."

"I yelled at you before." I try a smile. It doesn't take.

She looks up at me. "Why do you have to change?"

Because my brain is being eaten away and eventually there'll be nothing left of me, not the Dad you remember from before I got the disease, not the Dad I am now, not even the Dad I'll become as my symptoms worsen. Nothing.

I shrug. "That's just the way it is."

Sophie pouts, indignant. "But that's not fair!"

"It's okay. It doesn't bother me so it shouldn't bother you."

She frowns. Squatting down in front of her I try to think of a way to explain it.

"You remember you were upset last week because you couldn't go to the cinema with your friends?"

"Yeah."

"Well, you're not upset anymore, are you? You remember being upset but it's kind of vague, you're too caught up in the mood you're in now to really think about it. That's what it's like for me."

Sophie digests this, carefully mulling over what I've just said. Finally she speaks. "You should've let me go to the pictures. All my friends went."

Maybe I should've picked an example from longer than a week ago. "But you understand what I'm saying?"

She screws up her eyes in concentration. "… I think so."

"Good." I ruffle her hair.

"Daddy…"

"Yes?"

"Can I sleep with you and Mummy tonight?"

I look longingly at the canvas and then sigh. "I don't see why not."

Sophie takes my hand as I turn out the garage lights.

*

"Still can't get over Craig's paintings," says Justin. "They're amazing."

Paula and Zoë exchange glances, sure that my head will swell from the praise, expanding to fill the entire lounge.

Zoë gave me a lift back from the meditation class. When Justin mentioned he was taking the bus due to his car sitting at home with a flat battery Zoë offered him a lift too. Two cups of tea later and the pair of them are still here. Paula bounces Sophie on her knee, glad of the company. She doesn't get out as much as she used to. Not since I became ill. But she seems a little *too* glad of Justin's company. She keeps smiling at him, running her fingers through her hair, in full flirting mode.

She's wasting her time; it's obvious that he's still hung up on Zoë.

Justin looks at me over his teacup. "And you'd never done any painting before?"

"No. Everybody who gets Pick's disease changes their behaviour but only a tiny handful of sufferers gain new abilities. I'm one of the lucky ones."

Cautious glances flick between the others. No one's quite sure whether to agree with me or not.

I throw Sophie a wink and she beams back at me. She seems okay since our chat the other night. Things always seem worse in the middle of the night.

Paula looks at the clock on the mantelpiece. "It's past your bedtime, young lady."

"Oh, Mum." Sophie gives the last word a couple of dozen extra vowels as she runs it up and down the scales. "I've got something I wanted to tell everyone."

"Go on, then. But be quick."

Sophie hops off Paula's knee and looks round at us all, full of the self-importance that tells all young children that they are the centre of the universe. "I just wanted to tell you all –" a wicked grin flashes across her face and she blows the biggest raspberry I've ever heard in my life "– *phhhhlllbbbttt!!!*"

She bursts into high-pitched joyous laughter. Justin and Zoë join in. Paula's torn between laughing and being furious. "Go to bed, young lady! Now!"

I don't laugh, not because I see anything wrong in what Sophie's done but just because I don't think it's funny.

Sophie runs off to her room, still laughing.

Paula blushes. "She's a right little madam lately."

Paula might be more worried about Sophie if I'd told her about our chat the other night. But I haven't. After all, Paula never told me about the conversation she'd had with Sophie about me changing. So she thinks Sophie slept in our bed because of nightmares.

Justin chuckles. "Don't worry, I like to see children enjoy themselves. I appreciate their spontaneity."

"What's that Zen parable you told me?" asks Zoë. "The monk who gets attacked by bandits. Just as they swing their swords at him his Zen training allows him to respond totally spontaneously, he's living totally in the moment, and he screams in pure terror."

I scratch my chin. "If someone attacked me with a sword *I'd* scream. Does that mean I'm enlightened?"

"I don't think Justin's *that* good a teacher," says Paula. "You've only had three lessons."

Justin sips his tea. "Actually Craig's making amazing progress."

She leans over to him, giggling, toying with her hair, practically climbing onto his dick. "You're only saying that because he's buttering you up, inviting you round here for cups of tea."

Justin laughs politely. I cut across it. "You're the one who invited him in."

Paula's face wobbles. Just for a second. "So exactly what form of meditation do you teach, Justin?"

"It's a synthesis of various disciplines. Yoga, Zen Buddhism, Taoism, shamanism, Tantra." He glances over at Zoë at this last one and she blushes.

"Shamanism?" Paula frowns. "Isn't that like magic?"

"That's one way of describing it, yes."

I haven't heard about this part of the curriculum. Neither has Paula. Her body stiffens. "I'm sorry, I don't believe you should be teaching people that sort of thing."

Zoë and I both know what's coming. Zoë rolls her eyes. I settle back to enjoy the show.

Justin looks puzzled. "Why's that, exactly?"

"Because it's an affront to God."

He smiles. "I'm not a Satanist, you know."

"But shamanism does involve worshipping other gods?"

"Mmm... worshipping is probably too strong a word. More like *respecting* other gods."

"Why didn't you tell us this at that first class? Zoë must've told you we're Christians."

"I said not to tell you about that part of it," says Zoë. "Not until you'd had a chance to see how beneficial the class is."

Paula glares daggers at Zoë. Justin comes to Zoë's rescue. "I've not taught Craig any techniques that conflict with your faith. Everything he's done has been totally about self-actualisation. Strictly no mumbo-jumbo."

"That's all very well but –"

"If you want I can focus purely on Christian methods of meditation; contemplation, hesychasm. That sort of thing."

Paula shakes her head. "I don't even know what those are."

Me neither. But I've noticed Justin likes to show off exactly how much he knows about this stuff.

"I can give you some literature if you like," he says. "I'd intended to incorporate them into Craig's personal meditation programme anyway. If you don't like them then we'll call it quits." He gives her a twinkly-eyed smile. "What do you say?"

Paula fiddles with the cross about her neck, caught between Justin's charm and her faith. "We don't want anything to do with magic."

This has gone on long enough. Time to put my foot down. "If I want to take the class then I'll take the bloody class, you stupid cow."

Paula glowers at me. I know she wants to say more but for some reason she keeps quiet.

Justin and Zoë get up. "Er… we'd best be off. Zoë has to take a bit of a detour to drop me off at my place."

Paula and I see them to the door. No one says anything. I shake Justin's hand. "I'll see you next week then?" Justin's okay so long as he keeps away from Paula. And I enjoy his classes.

He glances at Paula then grins at me. The grin looks kind of tight. "'Bye."

Zoë gives me the same strained grin. "I'll talk to you later, okay?"

Paula shoots her a dirty look. "Goodbye."

She shuts the front door.

I go to speak to Paula but she turns away from me and walks up the stairs without saying a word.

*

The lines fill my vision.

Black blocks of ink, bisected by a fine mesh of crosshatching that twists into a parabola. And the stippling, a sprinkle of dots that adds texture, defining light and shade in a way that seems impossible for a few spots of ink to achieve.

I wonder what brushes were used to produce the pattern.

But then I remember Justin told me not to focus on that aspect of things. "Don't analyse the mandala. *Become* the mandala."

Even after his argument with Paula I'm not sure if this meditation exercise is strictly Christian. But I don't care. Everyone else in the class is doing it and I don't want to miss out.

Besides, he gave me that mantra to run through my head and that's definitely Christian. The Jesus Prayer from hesychasm, like the old Eastern Orthodox monks used to use. Kyrie eleison or, if you're not into Greek, 'Lord Jesus Christ, Son of God, have mercy on me a sinner'.

"Meditate on your personal mantra and the mandala at the same time." That's what Justin said. "Get your brain to operate on different levels simultaneously. There are different levels to spirituality, different dimensions."

My mandala certainly has many dimensions. It folds in and out, over and under itself in a manner that would give Escher a headache. The basic shape is of two Bs standing back to back, creating a mirror image of each other. But there's much more to it than that, layers of background detail adding in levels of intricate complexity.

And even the basic shape holds a multitude of identities, the lines suggesting different possibilities: a butterfly; a pair of amoeba splitting apart from each other; a heart breaking in two; a pair of superstrings vibrating at the subatomic level of the universe.

But then the shapes fade. The mandala goes blank, all of its features replaced by a blinding light. I try to turn to Justin or one of the other students but I'm stuck in place. All I can do is stare at that searing, blinding light and pray that it doesn't melt my retinas.

A cry for help never makes it past my lips. The only words I can think of hammer through my head. Kyrie eleison. Kyrie eleison. Kyrie eleison.

And then even that is gone.

Something looms before me in the light. Vast. Unknowable.

Slowly the light fades. Vision returns. My flesh is cool again, the skin unmarred by heat or flame.

I turn and stare at Justin and the other students. They continue with their meditation, oblivious.

They have no idea what just happened. What I just saw.

The face of God.

*

> *"I often feel a terrible need of – shall I say the word? – of religion.*
> *Then I go out and paint the stars."*
> *Vincent van Gogh*

"Calm down," says Justin. "It's not what you think it is."

"Calm down? How am I supposed to calm down? I've just seen God!"

Zoë hands me a cup of tea. "Stop bouncing around for five minutes and listen0 to what Justin has to say." As we're in Justin's flat I expect the tea to be some soothing herbal infusion. So I'm pleasantly surprised by the tang of brandy.

Justin gestures to an armchair. "Take a seat."

I sit. Zoë takes the seat next to me. Justin remains standing, there's no more chairs. The décor in the flat is sparse, minimalist. He's probably had the place feng shuied.

"What you experienced has many names: theoptia, unio mystica, but there are scientific explanations for it. Meditation affects the parietal lobe, the part of the brain that controls body image and the sense of time and space inhabited by the body. That's why meditators feel they're floating, that they've achieved a sense of oneness with the universe. It's not some great cosmic awakening, it's just that they're not registering their own bodies the way they would normally."

"Bollocks!" I snap. "I saw God!"

Justin raises an eyebrow. "So what does God look like?"

"He…" I don't have the words. I don't think the words even exist. "Give me something to draw with."

Justin hands me a pen and notepad. I start scribbling.

Okay, a curve here, and then straight lines leading to a corner – no, the perspective's all wrong. But if I foreshorten this bit, change the proportions slightly – no, it still doesn't work. Right, break it down into units; cubes, spheres, cones. And now this bit – er, no, that star effect wasn't part of His face. Except that it was.

I fling the pad onto the coffee table. My aborted attempt to draw God looks like something Picasso might have produced whilst tripping. "I can't show you what it was like. You have to see it for yourself."

Zoë reaches over and strokes my arm. "Don't worry, people occasionally get visions when they're meditating. It's not a big deal. You've just got to ignore them."

Justin picks up the pad. "Zoë's right. In Zen they call it *makyo*. Illusions and hallucinations that creep into your meditation practice. The trick is not to get seduced by them." He looks at the mess of lines and scribbles on the pad and something flickers across his face. "Nice drawing. Bit abstract for my tastes though."

I slouch in the armchair, annoyed at being beaten. "I thought I could draw anything."

"Yeah," says Zoë, "but God's too fidgety to be a good subject for a portrait. He keeps moving in mysterious ways."

Justin sits on the edge of the coffee table, bringing himself onto my eye level. "Look, this probably won't happen again but maybe you should take some private lessons instead of the regular classes. That way I can help guide you through any rough patches."

My cynicism rears its head. "And how much do *they* cost?"

"First one's free. See if you think it's helping you."

"Okay. I'll give it a go."

Justin rubs his chin, embarrassed. "And it might be an idea to not mention this to Paula. If it's a one-off there's no point in getting her upset."

Whatever. All I care about right now is getting to see God again.

*

The sky is cornflower blue, clouds as white as daisy petals. The sun shines, I feel its touch upon my skin; hot, heavy. The white flesh of my legs seems brighter under the shining rays, almost as if reflecting the sunlight; I could probably act as a heliograph, flashing messages far into the distance.

Margaret Wharton walks by carrying a tub of scones she bought at one of the fete's stalls. She pulls her sunglasses down her nose so she can get a better look at my shorts. "Oo, nice legs. If I was twenty years younger…"

Margaret is one of the few people who seems to have genuinely forgiven me for my latest outburst in the church. They all *pretend* to have forgiven me – it's the Christian thing to do – but some of them would rather I steered clear of the church. They view me as a social time bomb, ready to spray them with *faux pas* shrapnel at any moment.

Especially after I told them that I'd seen God.

Justin was probably right, I should've kept quiet about it but when Reverend Palmer started droning on about "Thou canst not see my face: for there shall no man see me and live" I couldn't help myself. I jumped up and told them about my vision.

Some of them were fascinated, others were horrified. Blasphemy. Sacrilege. Heresy. How could I claim to have seen God whilst trapped in some heathen meditation?

I told them to fuck off.

They didn't catch what I said, the words lost in the babble of voices, the towering swell of curiosity and outrage. Paula said afterwards that this was a good thing but I don't see why, I was just adding my thoughts to a healthy debate.

I look down at the paints on my stall. I thought more of the kids would want their faces painted. But since Paula got called away to help with the tombola hardly anyone has come over to the stall. Too scared to talk to the brain damaged heretic.

Bored, I munch on a tortilla.

Sophie walks by with a group of her friends. I wave to her. "Sophie! You want your face painted?"

Giggling, she runs over. Her friends follow her. Sophie jumps up and down in front of the stall. "Give me a tiger face!"

"Okay. And after that I'll paint your friends' faces."

Her friends shift their feet uncomfortably at my suggestion.

Sophie finally settles down enough for me to paint her face without risking poking her in the eye. Once the orange base is laid I toss in the whiskers and the black stripes. The painting takes over my hands; swift, deft strokes that give Sophie's face a stern beauty that shouldn't be possible merely by daubing paint on an eight year old.

Sophie looks up at me. "Did you really see God, Daddy?"

"Yes."

She glances over at her friends. They all share the same look of horrified fascination. Suddenly I realise that I'm here as a side-show freak.

I continue painting, reading Sophie's character; I capture her wants, her desires, her loves, her hates. The depths of her soul bleed through onto her face.

"If you've seen God can you ask Him for world peace?" she asks.

"I think you'd have to ask Him for something smaller than that."

Squinting, she thinks for a moment. Then she brightens. "How about if I asked Him for a DVD player?"

"Heh. Nice try."

Finishing the painting I turn Sophie round so her friends can see her face.

They all stare at her in silence. Their faces shift, unsure what it is they're looking at. Then one of them starts crying. One runs away, screaming for her parents.

They're just jealous that none of them are as beautiful as Sophie.

*

Paula walks into the garage, drying her hands on a towel. "I finally managed to get that muck off her face."

I grunt a reply, too engrossed in my painting to really pay attention.

"You should've waited for me to come back before doing any face painting."

I dip my brush into my palette. "Why? I didn't do anything wrong."

Paula doesn't reply and I think she's left the garage so I just continue with my painting, focusing my attention on the canvas. Then: "You were talking about seeing God again weren't you?"

Her voice has that tight, controlled sound to it that she gets whenever she's fighting to keep her temper. Like a wire stretched so tight it's about to snap.

Lowering my brush I turn to face her. "I'm not going to lie to people about it, all right?"

She stands, features stern, arms folded, the towel dangling from her fingers like a sash. Her folded arms frame her breasts, accentuating the small mounds of soft flesh, and suddenly I want to squeeze them together and thrust my cock in the warm cleft between them until I come.

She frowns. "I want you to at least consider the idea that it was an optical illusion. Like that pattern you can get off the Internet where the shapes turn into the face of Jesus."

I've already had this argument with Justin. Random sights and sounds can sometimes take on significant meaning for the observer – voices hidden on records, faces on tortillas. Of course he had a fancy name for it: pareidolia. "That still doesn't explain the way I felt. The feeling of wonder, the feeling of awe."

"I get that feeling every time I go to church!" snaps Paula. "And so did you before –" She stops, her face crumpling. Then she slips her mask of weary control back on. "Just stop and think before you say anything, okay? Even if you can't see anything wrong with what you're about to say – stop."

I frown. "Look, as far as I'm concerned I'm not doing anything wrong. There's plenty of other people out there acting like arseholes who *know* they're arseholes. Why don't you go complain about them?"

"Because I'm not married to them." The hand holding the towel clenches and unclenches. "I don't love them. I love you."

I smile. "Good."

That seems like the right thing to say but Paula just stares at me, as though waiting for something more, some sort of deeper reply. Unsure what to do, I say nothing.

Eventually Paula looks away, rubbing a hand to her tired brow. "You know Sophie's playing up to your illness?"

"How d'you mean?"

"She keeps getting out of classes at school, saying she's too stressed out because of having to deal with you being ill. She insults the teachers, bullies the other kids but then puts on the puppy dog eyes and says, 'But my dad's ill.'"

I scratch my nose with the end of my paintbrush. "And the teachers are stupid enough to let her get away with this?"

"They've spoken to her but there's only so much they can do. Sophie's teacher Miss Roberts had a quick chat with me about it on Friday but we need to have a proper discussion, work out how much of it is genuine and how much is her trying it on."

"Right. What time are we meeting Miss Roberts?"

"*I'm* meeting her Monday afternoon. If you're there it'll be easier for Sophie to convince Miss Roberts that she really does need to be treated with kid gloves. Besides, the other kids will tease her if they see you acting funny."

My cheeks burn. "I don't act funny."

Paula counts off points on her fingers. "You're rude. You insult people. You stare at women like they're pieces of meat. You reduce children to tears. And, oh yeah, you claim to have seen God."

"But –"

"And then there's this." She gestures to my painting.

I look at my picture, hurt that she seems offended by it. The picture shows bodies. Live bodies, dead bodies, deformed bodies.   All naked.

Paraplegics copulate with dwarves; shivering Aids victims use the entrails of dead children as blankets. The bodies interlock with one another, producing a larger picture, creating a face. The decapitated head of an elderly black man becomes a nostril. The pale, withered body of a dying leper becomes an eyebrow. A chorus line of female amputees offer their vaginas as the face's lips; their stubby legs spread, sprayed with semen, forming a beard and moustache. All human emotion is here; love, hope, joy, despair, fear, regret. All contained within a single face. God's face.

It's a good painting. In fact it's a great painting. But it doesn't even come close to capturing the reality.

"That thing would give Hieronymous Bosch nightmares. What's it supposed to be?"

Hurt at this confirmation of how poor my effort is and upset at being kept out of the loop of Sophie's problems at school I find myself lost for words.

"So I think it's a good idea if you don't go to the school with me, yes?"

I don't say anything.

"Good." Paula rubs her temple again. "Jesus, I'm getting a migraine."

"Come here." Putting my palette to one side I start stroking her head. Zoë's always raving about the Indian Head Massages Justin used to give her. Never tried it myself but it seems easy enough. My fingers caress Paula's skin, the movement natural, flowing.

With a tiny sigh of pleasure Paula melts beneath my hands.

My thoughts turn to other things. Paula, Sophie, seeing God. Things are getting complicated. Or was life always like this and I just accepted it before?

*

Justin uses a different room in the sports centre for his private lessons. Smaller, probably a way to keep the hire costs down. Still, Zoë tells me he charges fifty pounds per hour so the cost of hiring a room can't dent his wallet *that* badly.

My bus is late, so he's already there when I arrive. I wish that Paula would let me use my car. She reckons I'm a menace, that I keep pulling out from junctions without looking, but I've never actually caused an accident. Well, there was that one time, but you can't really call that an accident, none of the cars involved were write-offs.

As I hurry towards the room Justin's hired I can see him through the window. He's doing some kind of moving meditation, gliding forward and back, weight shifting from the ball of his foot back to his heel; then he twists and turns, his arms moving in slow, graceful swirls before him, switching between circles and straight lines. He looks like a ballroom dancer forced to practice the steps solo until their partner arrives.

As I enter the room he slides to a graceful halt and smiles a greeting. "Hi."

"Missed my bus."

He nods. "Thought it was something like that. It's not as if you can ask Paula for a lift is it?"

My eyes narrow slightly. Was that a dig? After our argument over the face painting I told Paula I'd stop going to Justin's class. The fact that he conducts private lessons on a different day to his regular classes helps disguise the lie.

Besides, Paula's happy with me right now. The Indian Head Massage cured her migraine. My touch eased her pain, turning it into something else and we ended up screwing all night. Paula moaned and groaned in ecstasy as my fingers danced over her clitoris. Foreplay isn't normally my favourite part of sex but this time I got a kick out of it. The tips of my fingers traced out the face of God onto Paula's clitoris. The impossibility of following such an intricate pattern forced my fingers to approach her from angles I never even knew existed. Could barely move my hand by the time she came. Gave me a thrill knowing I was pleasuring her with something she was so dead set against.

A smile flickers across my face at the memory.

"What's so funny?" Justin's question brings me back to the present.

"Nothing." I watch as Justin stretches his arms out behind him, opening up his chest muscles. "What was that you were doing when I came in?"

"Taiji. Different pronunciation of tai chi."

I shake my head, amused. "How many different types of meditation do you study?"

"Taiji's not just about meditation. It's –" he cocks his head to one side, trying to think of the perfect explanation "– it's about becoming the embodiment of yin and yang. There's a spiritual side to the art; a healing side; a combative side."

"Combative? Learning Chinese mime teaches you how to fight?"

He smiles. "If you learn it correctly. The solo form contains a vast array of fighting techniques but it takes other training methods such as pushing hands and free sparring to teach you how to apply the techniques. And the correct mental attitude of course. Utilising the reptile brain."

He's showing off, eager to show how clever he is, but I'm curious. "Reptile brain?"

"Yes. Certain postures help access the older, more instinctive part of the brain. It's similar to how smiling triggers certain parts of the brain to make you feel better. So if you adopt the correct pose –" he raises his hands to a guard position, allows his shoulders to round off into a smooth curve "– it accesses the brainstem, the reptile brain. Your vision changes, you respond to movement differently. Something breaches your personal space you attack it. Or, more accurately, intercept your attacker's attack with one of your own."

He pats me on the shoulder. "Don't worry, that isn't what we'll be doing."

My face tightens. Does this arsehole think I'm scared of him?

Justin picks up a towel and wipes the light sheen of sweat from his brow. I notice a fine tracery of scars along his forearms, the puckered flesh virtually hidden beneath his black tattoos. "Where'd you get the scars?"

He pauses, lowers the towel slowly. "Someone pulled a knife on me once."

Turning, he puts his towel in his sports bag. He obviously doesn't want to talk about it.

"Looks nasty. They cut you up pretty bad." Don't bolster your ego on me, dickhead. I'm not scared of you.

"Yeah." Justin turns back to me. "That's why I got the tattoos. To cover them up."

"Pretty drastic. A tattoo's for life."

"Yeah, well, so are the scars."

I shrug. "S'pose."

The topic hangs in the air, not quite ended but not quite ready for further discussion. I let the silence drag for another half second so Justin thinks I've let it drop then I hit him again. "Your taiji wasn't much use to you there, was it?"

"Depends on your definition of useful." He looks at me. "I took most of the cuts on my arms but one thrust got through and punctured my lung. I was in hospital for months. If I hadn't stopped the other thrusts I would've died."

I rub my chin then step up close to him. "So how good are you then? What if I tried to punch you in the mouth?"

He doesn't even blink. "I'm good enough to stop you. But I'm not good enough to do it without hurting you."

Behind his glasses his eyes go hard. Like steel shutters dropping into place. All his touchy-feely New Age stuff flies out the window. Doesn't matter what happens, he'll do whatever he has to.

I step back out of range. "I'd better not try to punch you in the mouth then."

The steel shutters remain in place.

I pull my mandala from my pocket. "Right. Let's see if you can get me to see God again shall we?"

*

Zoë's scissors snip at my hair.

As she moves round me her breasts brush against the back of my head. It feels nice. I remember when her breasts used to be mine to fondle. Happy days. Still, good as we were together we're better as friends. Zoë never wanted to settle down or have kids. Most women worry about their biological clock but Zoë's came fitted with a snooze button.

I thought maybe her recently discovered New Age tendencies might awaken her maternal instincts but no, she still thinks the best children are those that have been locked in a trunk and then dumped at the bottom of the ocean.

Zoë measures my hair through her fingers. "So how'd your lesson with Justin go?"

"I saw God again. But He looked… different. I mean, He was the same, but He wasn't. I don't know how to describe it." Beneath the apron that stops my hair falling on the carpet of Zoë's flat I give an exasperated shrug. "Justin went on about *makyo* and pseudo-nirvanas and a whole bunch of other stuff I didn't understand."

Zoë chuckles. "Yeah, that sounds like Justin."

"He kept saying how dangerous this could be and that I should only meditate under his supervision." I've ignored his advice, I meditate whenever I can. But I can't always get to see God.

I glance round Zoë's flat. Jackie Collins novels nestle alongside her copy of *The Alchemist*. An unsmoked joint sits atop a stack of back issues of *Cosmopolitan*. And the posters: Orson Welles glares out from beneath his black slouch hat and cloak; *Forbidden Planet*'s Robby the Robot cradles an unconscious Anne Francis in his arms; a print of a Tarot card is reflected in a mirror on the far wall, showing Adam and Eve standing naked before the Tree of Knowledge, the serpent entwined around its trunk. They look happy, life must have been wonderful before they ate the apple, their idyllic relationship with God yet to be shattered by tainted knowledge.

"Did you tell Paula about seeing God?" asks Zoë.

"Yeah. Didn't tell her where though. She still doesn't like anyone but her precious church to have any claim on God." I look at up Zoë. "Is this why you wanted to cut my hair here instead of at the salon? You're worried someone will report back to Paula about me still taking the classes?"

Zoë puts a hand to her chest, feigning shock. "Are you suggesting that people in hair salons gossip? I'm deeply offended." She gently twists my head so that I face forwards again. "Now keep still unless you want to end up like van Gogh."

I sniff. "My paintings are better than his."

"So modest." Zoë giggles. "Did you know van Gogh got chucked out of a monastery for being too religious? Drove the monks to distraction apparently."

I go quiet, silently sympathising with old Vincent.

"He had temporal lobe epilepsy," says Zoë. "Gave him all kinds of mystical visions and stuff."

I raise an eyebrow. "You been talking to Justin? He's the one who normally comes out with all the trivia."

She sighs. "I know. He doesn't know when to stop."

"That why you dumped him?"

"One of the reasons. Part of it was the sex. Tantra's great but after awhile the rituals get a bit tedious. And I always felt kind of insulted that I never made him come."

She leans in and I smell her perfume. She wouldn't have any problems making me come.

"Anyway, I've been looking things up on the Net for you. Stuff connected with people who've seen God."

"Yeah? Find anything?"

"Well, there's tons of stuff out there but I still haven't managed to wade through it all to find what's relevant to you. I know you're a bit stuck when it comes to using the Net."

Another side effect of the Pick's. A few years back I was a certified mouse potato but now I struggle to open my emails.

"Thanks, Zoë."

She pauses, the scissors half-open, and smiles. "What are friends for?"

Reaching out from beneath the apron I pat her bum, then squeeze. "You're the best."

She tilts her head. "Did you want me to finish doing your hair or not?"

"Right." My hand retreats beneath the apron. Zoë continues cutting my hair, pretending nothing has happened.

But she's still smiling.

*

"I'm worried that you might harm yourself unless I help guide you through the meditation."

Justin has his best earnest face on, his hands held out to me; open, friendly.

My own hands wave in frustration. "Don't be stupid. Visions aren't going to hurt me, are they Zoë?"

25

Zoë looks up from where she's gazing out through the window, admiring the muscles on the bodybuilders in the room opposite us as they pump iron. "Ask Justin. He's the expert."

Justin rests a caring hand on my shoulder. "There are lots of different things bubbling away in a person's subconscious. Freud talked about the Id, with Jung it was the Shadow, the dark side of our nature. I just want to make sure you don't start hallucinating images of your repressed emotions whilst you're meditating."

"Have you listened to Craig talk?" asks Zoë. "He doesn't *have* any repressed emotions."

"Please." Justin looks at me, bleeding sincerity and compassion. "I need to know nothing's going to hurt you whilst you're meditating."

Part of me wants to storm out of there; I can meditate at home. But part of me wants someone else to see God, to know I'm not just imagining it. "If we do this you'll be seeing what I see?"

Justin nods. "To a certain extent. We'll both be following the same cues to guide our meditation although obviously we'll interpret them in different ways. But as far as you're concerned I'll be floating alongside you in your meditation. If you get into trouble I can help guide you back to full consciousness."

"But we'll still be separate? You won't actually *be* in my vision."

He grins. "Maybe. Maybe not."

His eyes slide over to Zoë as he speaks and I realise his words are for her benefit, not mine. Trying to impress her with his tricks, hoping she'll come back to him.

"Right," I say. "I suppose we'd better get on with it then. This is costing me money."

Justin and I sit cross-legged in front of my mandala. I glance across at him and just for a second I see the tightness in his face. He doesn't want to do this. A few seconds of pranayama breathing to calm himself and he focuses his attention on my mandala. I do likewise. I don't expect this to work but then again when I first started meditating I never expected to see God.

It only takes a few seconds for the world to recede around me. The mandala and the words of the hesychasm swirl, become one. I join them. Beside me I get a vague impression of Justin but he seems lost, confused.

I call across to him. Don't be afraid.

He doesn't hear me.

A light starts to glow ahead of us. Dim at first but growing steadily brighter. Soon the light fills the horizon, fills me, fills the whole of creation. God is here.

He has no face this time, no definite features, but I can sense gradations to the light, the different wavelengths corresponding to different emotions, different expressions.

It's wonderful. I want to stay here forever.

Suddenly the light vanishes and I'm back in the real world. Zoë and Justin and the clamminess of the plastic mat beneath me and the faint smell of stale sweat in the air. It all seems so dull, so empty.

"What happened?" I ask. "Why did it end so quick?"

"Quick?" Zoë raises an eyebrow. "You were under for nearly an hour."

"You're joking!" I look at my watch. She's right.

I pat Justin on the shoulder. "Well, did you see it? Did you see God?"

He still has the confused expression he wore in the vision. "I saw something. I'm not sure what it was."

"It was God! You must've seen it!"

He shakes his head as though trying to wake from a bad dream. "It wasn't quite clear…"

"We'll have to do it again. You'll get a better look next time."

"Yeah. Maybe." He picks up his sports bag. "I'm going to hit the showers. Call me when you want another lesson."

He hurries from the room as though eager to escape from the memory of the vision he's just experienced.

*

Dr Carling's office is so tidy it frightens me. I suppose being a doctor and everything he's probably got a very disciplined mind but the gleaming polished surface of his desk, the neatly stacked pile of files that look so crisp and fresh I suspect they've been ironed, it's not natural.

I would blame this hyper-cleanliness on his cleaner but Dr Carling himself is always so impeccably turned out. The crease down the front of his trousers is so sharp you could use it as a letter opener and it wouldn't surprise me to find he tucked his shirt in using hospital corners

Thank God for the photos on his desk. Him in a dirty T-shirt and crumpled shorts, laughing as he rolled around the lawn with his two sons, regardless of the grass stains he got on his clothes. The man is human after all.

But still I find myself trying not to slouch as Paula and I sit in his office waiting for him to return with the results of my latest MRI scan.

Being slid into the MRI chamber always makes me feel like I'm a torpedo being loaded into a torpedo tube. Or, if I'm feeling Freudian, a penis entering a vagina.

Of course that gets me thinking about last night. Paula's been far more passionate in bed recently. Maybe she's just using sex to compensate for the way she feels about my illness, throwing all her frustrated energies into her lovemaking, but she's definitely more responsive. I had a momentary irrational worry that the MRI would pick up my memories of our love marathon but then I decided that even if the machine did somehow suddenly become sensitive enough to pick up my thoughts it was nothing to be ashamed of. I'd been great in bed last night, why not brag about it?

I look at Paula. She seems kind of tense, fingers drumming on the arm of her chair. As I look at her an idea forms. Sex on Carling's desk. Our sweaty skin smearing the polish, our thrashing limbs and thrusting hips scattering the neatly ordered notes and papers, defiling his desk.

The thrill of desecration overwhelms me and I feel myself harden. But before I can suggest the idea Paula speaks.

"How many times have you seen God now?"

As I give my answer I wonder how long it will take for us to start rowing. "Three times."

She nods. She already knew the answer, I've told her every time I've seen God. "But it's only when you meditate?"

"Yeah. I have to focus on the mandala."

Paula looks away, the tempo of her fingers upon the arm of the chair increases. Then she looks back at me. "What's it like?"

The most difficult question. The unanswerable question. I sat up one night with a dictionary listing all the words I could find that captured the sensation. I ended up with over a thousand words but still didn't have an accurate description of the experience.

"It's... like nothing on earth. Imagine the most intense sensation you've ever experienced then multiply it by a million. That *almost* describes the way I feel *after* the sensation has nearly faded."

"And you've never felt that way during prayer?"

"No." I scratch my nose. "But then again most people don't feel that way during meditation."

Paula nods, slowly, thoughtfully. "You know how I've always known God exists?"

I shake my head.

"When I was young I had a pen-pal in Australia. Never met her but I knew she existed because I'd get her letters. It was the same sort of thing with God, I knew I'd never meet Him but I knew He existed because I could read His words in the Bible, I could even read His purpose in the way my prayers were answered. I thought that was the sort of relationship all believers had with God. But then you start seeing Him and I want to believe it's God but you're ill and you're only seeing Him when you're using a kind of worship that's totally alien to me."

She folds her arms, hugging herself tightly.   To her normally unshakeable faith her words are tantamount to blasphemy.   She sits waiting for a thunderbolt to strike her.

The door to the office opens and Dr Carling comes in. His face is red, flustered. "I just looked at your MRI results."

"And?"

He glances down at the photo in his hand as if reluctant to show it to us.   Then he hands it over, apologetic.   "I have absolutely no idea what that is. Never seen anything like it."

Paula and I look at the brain scan. Then we look at each other. Paula's face is full of shock.   So is mine.

Superimposed over the image of my brain is a picture of my mandala.

*

> *"Tiger, tiger, burning bright*
> *In the forests of the night,*
> *What immortal hand or eye*
> *Could frame thy fearful symmetry?"*
> *William Blake*

"So," says Zoë, "do you want to hear what else I found?"

"I suppose. That *is* why I came round."

She chuckles. "Right. That's why it's taken half an hour to get round to the subject."

"That's your fault."

She props herself up on her elbow. "How do you work that out?"

"You seduced me."

"Hah!"

When I headed off for Zoë's flat all I'd intended was to look at the information she'd gathered. That, and to tell her about the mandala on my brain scan. After seeing it I told Dr Carling about my visions of God. He said it might be a stimulation of the temporal lobes, there were several cases of people experiencing mystical visions after these lobes had been stimulated. He was annoyed that we hadn't mentioned it sooner. And he was even more annoyed when he couldn't pinpoint any definite signs of temporal lobe stimulation; the mandala obscured his view. Although he'd cheered up a little by the time we left. He didn't say anything but I think he's planning a paper on my visions.

That's what I wanted to talk to Zoë about.   The mandala and her findings.

But the bus on the way over was crowded. Trapped in the press of the passengers I found myself jammed up against a pensioner. She was fat – old people always either wither away to nothing or else balloon as though they'd been crossbred with an inflatable dinghy – and wrinkled and grey. Not to mention the musky odour that hung over her – 'Incontinence' by Calvin Klein. But still, I don't know if it was because she was pressed up against me so tight or if it was the motion of the bus but I found myself getting aroused.

So by the time I got to Zoë's I was already feeling pretty horny. And then she opened the door in her tight gym wear, sweat glistening on her legs and cleavage. "Just doing some extra yoga," she said.

The Lycra shorts hugged her arse as she walked into her lounge. The wiggle of those rounded buttocks was too much. I took them in my hands and squeezed. She jumped, caught by surprise. Then I kissed her, grabbing at her arse again.

She kissed me back.

Now, in the post-coital glow, she nudges me in the ribs. "You did all the chasing."

"Yeah, but you wanted to be caught."

"True enough." She shifts uncomfortably in the bed, taking the pressure off her sore buttocks. "Just didn't expect to get caught there. You never used to be into that sort of thing."

I lean back against the pillows, my hands behind my head, and a ring of Zoë's shit around the end of my dick. Good job she had vaseline in her medicine cabinet. "Anyway, what was it you said you'd found out?"

Zoë snuggles up to me, I can smell that fancy shampoo she uses. "What do you want first, the exciting stuff or the trivia?"

"Well, I know how you like to build slowly to a climax –" she slaps my shoulder "– so let's start with the trivia.'

"Okay. This isn't really relevant but it caught my eye. There's an archaeologist called Steven Mithen who reckons that religion came into being around 60,000 years ago, about the same time as art and technology. He says that as prehistoric humans evolved different parts of their minds started to overlap – the bit connected with hunting, the bit connected with communication and whatever – so that they could imagine things as having more than one purpose or meaning. So, like, a tree branch could be used as a spear, a splodge of mud on a cave wall became a picture of a deer, and then that picture became the symbol of say, the god of hunting."

I raise an eyebrow. "And this relates to me how exactly?"

"Well, it's just that you didn't start seeing God until after you started doing art so it just struck me as a bit of a coincidence. And the technology fits in with you fixing cars." She strokes my chest. "But that's where it all falls down because you can't do that anymore."

I stare at the ceiling, suddenly morbid. I've lost my grip on technology and as the Pick's disease gets worse I'll lose the ability to paint and draw. Does that mean I'm going to eventually lose God as well?

"Forget it," says Zoë. "It's a stupid idea. I just liked the sound of it."

"So what was the other thing you found?"

"You'll like this." Zoë climbs up onto her knees, excited as a kid at Christmas. Her naked breasts jiggle up and down as she moves. Picking her handbag up off the floor she pulls out a photo she's printed off the Internet. "Look familiar?"

The photo shows a copy of the picture I attempted to draw of God immediately after the first time I saw Him.

My heart quickens. "Where did you get this?"

"My Internet search took me to a New Age group. They're into all different types of meditation and stuff. They were all set to become the next big thing in the mind, body and spirit market. But the organisation had a setback after their guru started seeing visions of God." She taps the photo in my hand.

"Why was that a setback?"

"Because he went mad and killed himself."

I look at the photo. "That doesn't exactly cheer me up."

"Wait. I haven't told you the good bit yet." Zoë pauses, milking the moment. "At the time the guru went mad guess who was one of his chief disciples?"

I look at her.

She nods. "Justin."

*

I walk through the house, searching for a towel.

The airing cupboard is in mine and Paula's bedroom, a bad piece of house design that I've never got round to rectifying. As it is we have to suffer Sophie bounding into the room at all kinds of unearthly hours, searching for her favourite T-shirt or nightie. So the room serves as both boudoir and fashion boutique. And, with the overflowing washing basket in the corner it also houses dirty laundry. Not to mention the books on the bedside cabinet making it a reading room. My novel is *Tiger! Tiger!*, a tatty old SF paperback that I bought years ago but never got round to reading until now. Paula's book is the Bible. She's been reading it more than ever lately.

Taking a towel from the airing cupboard I dry my hands. The paint hasn't washed off my hands properly; a dark rainbow of blacks and greys streaks the cloth.

Much as I enjoy the painting I'd rather be talking to Justin, asking him exactly what kind of visions his guru had. And why they drove him mad.

But I haven't been able to get in touch with him. The last few days using the phone has become increasingly difficult for me. I keep forgetting exactly what I'm supposed to do to get the machine to connect me to the person I want to talk to. Or even what part of the phone I'm supposed to talk into. Pretty soon I won't even remember what the bloody thing's called.

So I painted instead. A cobweb of stars, stretching across infinity, circling each other in intricate patterns dictated by the invisible aesthetics of gravity.

But if you looked closer you could see another pattern, clusters of light and voids of blackness melding together to form shapes, a face. God's beatific visage, far more wondrous than mere humans could ever imagine; benign, serene. And yet somehow that is what sent a chill along my spine as I painted. The stars, those beacons of God's achievements, of His eternal majesty, were fading, dying, the edge of the canvas devoured by an encroaching blackness. The universe and everything in it was slowly decaying, disintegrating. And God didn't care.

I'd had to leave the canvas unfinished. My hands were shaking too much to continue.

Wiping the paint and water from my hands I head towards the bedroom door. As I move I notice one of the drawers is ajar in Paula's makeup table. The drawer where she keeps her diary.

Draping the towel over my shoulder I open the drawer and take out her diary. It's a leather-bound volume with a light sprinkling of gold along the pages' edge. Not just something for jotting down notes in, this is a solid, sturdy volume for recording all your deepest thoughts and emotions.

I start to read.

I thought I could cope. It was hard but I knew my love and my faith would see me through.

But now, with Craig's visions of God, I don't know whether to envy him or to hate him. Maybe the Lord really is appearing to him, offering him solace before taking him into His Kingdom. But somehow I can't believe that. My faith has always been in the small miracles, the way God's presence permeates the world with the freshness of a rainstorm, the fragile beauty of a tulip's petals, the way the ocean foams and roars as it crashes upon the shore.

But to actually see Him directly?

No. I can't fit the concept inside my mind. You only see God directly when you're dead, when you've ascended to Heaven. That's when we shed our human weaknesses, transforming into beings worthy of His love.

*When we truly awaken to His glory. Burning bushes are no longer viable.
God's moved on, He has shown us the way and now we must go to Him.*

*So I just try to cope with Craig's illness as best I can, praying quietly
to God to help see me through. Trying to ignore his worst excesses, just
try to clear up the mess after him and hope that when night falls he'll take
me to bed and fuck my brains out.*

*After twelve years of marriage I thought I knew what sex was supposed
to feel like. But now I realise there's so much more to it. What I'd
thought had been orgasms had just been the initial tremors, what I've
been experiencing lately is the full-blown earthquake, shooting right off
the Richter scale. It's only now I realise I mistook the pleasures of
regular sex for the thrill of orgasm.*

*And I wonder that if I was wrong about something so personal, so
intimate, then maybe I'm wrong about God, wrong about Heaven, wrong
about everything?*

Finishing the entry I lower the diary.

It never occurred to me that I might not have satisfied Paula in bed.
She was the innocent virgin on our wedding night not me – my old church
was much more lenient about pre-marital sex than hers. Still, if she
mistook even my regular humping for orgasms that must mean I'm pretty
damn good.

I hope.

I walk downstairs to the kitchen, flicking through the diary, trying to
find an entry that confirms my pre-foreplay sex as either fantastic or a
flop.

Entering the kitchen I find Paula pouring herself a glass of orange
juice. She stares at her diary. "What the hell are you doing with that?"

"Just reading about our sex life." I nod towards the pitcher in her
hand. "Could you pour me some juice?"

Paula's porcelain skin turns red, her eyebrows drawing into a scowl.
Oh hell, don't tell me this is another social taboo I've forgotten.

She snatches the diary from my hand. "You bastard!"

"What? I'm your husband, surely I'm allowed to read your diary."

"Of course you're not!" Her body twists, holding the diary as far
behind her as possible, as if afraid I might be able to read through its
cover if I get too close to it.

I try to explain. "But it's got stuff in there that you don't tell me
about."

"Exactly!"

"But I want to know about this stuff. We shouldn't have secrets."

"Do you tell me everything that you think about?"

"Of course I do."

"*Liar!*" She hurls the word at me with such ferocity that I flinch. "You don't tell me everything. And even if you did it wouldn't mean anything. You could tell me your deepest darkest secret and a couple of days later you wouldn't even care that you'd told me. It wouldn't be something you cared about anymore!"

I clench my fists. "That's not my fault, is it?"

"Oh, of course nothing's ever your fault!" She waves her hands above her head, the sarcasm spewing out of her. "Because you're ill, you can't be held responsible for acting like a selfish inconsiderate prick!" She glares at me. "Well, if it's not your fault then whose fault is it?"

"God's."

Her eyes narrow to an angry squint. "Don't you *dare* insult God in my house."

"At least I get to see God. You don't."

She stiffens. "How much of my diary did you read?"

"Enough to know that you're wondering whether you've wasted your life with all this church crap."

She snatches up her glass and hurls it at me. I duck. Cold juice spills over me as the glass sails over my head.

Behind me I hear the splintering of glass. And a scream.

As she stares over my shoulder the rage drains from Paula's face. It's replaced with horror.

Spinning round I see a mark on the wallpaper where the glass hit the wall, exploding, spraying the room with crystalline shards.

And beneath that I see Sophie lying sprawled on the carpet, a sliver of razor-sharp glass jutting from her throat.

*

"Oh God, oh Jesus, oh Jesus!"

Paula rushes over to Sophie, cradles her in her arms. Dazed, I follow her.

"Mummy," Sophie's voice cracks, making it even higher than usual. "Mummy, I'm scared."

"Don't be, darling." Tears well up in Paula's eyes as she speaks. "Everything's going to be all right."

Paula looks up at me, screams: "Phone an ambulance!"

I stare at her blankly. "Phone?"

"Over there!" She points to a tray studded with buttons and with what looks like a scrubbing brush lying on top. Running over I snatch up the tray. The brush comes loose, hanging from a cord. I notice the brush has no bristles.

How the hell does this thing help me call an ambulance?

I shout to Paula. "What do I do?"

Her mouth drops open. "Bring it over here!"

I run over to her, carrying the tray.

She lays Sophie back on the floor. "Mummy's going to phone an ambulance. You talk to Daddy now."

Snatching the tray from my hands she stabs at its buttons.

I look down at Sophie. Blood trickles from the edges of her wound. It's only a small amount of blood but it's thick, and so dark it's almost black. Sophie's eyes bulge with fear; frightened whimpers escape her mouth. Then her eyelids begin to drift slowly shut.

I shake her. "Stay awake!"

Her eyelids flutter open. Then they start to close again.

"Stay awake!"

Beside me I hear Paula babbling our address into the scrubbing brush.

Sophie's eyes become narrow slits.

"Stay awake, damn it! Or I'll shove this glass so far into your neck it'll come out the other side!"

She doesn't hear my threat, or if she does she can't respond. Half crazy with fear I decide to fake it. Placing one hand around the flesh surrounding the glass I raise my other hand high, as though about to hammer the glass into her throat. Please let this frighten her into staying awake. If this doesn't work I don't know what else to do.

I start to bring my hand down. Behind me Paula screams.

Then Sophie jerks beneath my other hand. Her eyes snap open and the glass falls from her wound. I flinch, expecting to get sprayed with blood now the glass isn't blocking her artery. But there's nothing. No wound, just a slight dent in her skin. As I watch even that fades, leaving my hand resting on unblemished skin.

Wriggling free of my grip Sophie runs to Paula and hugs her. Paula stares at her, touches her neck to make sure the wound really has vanished. Then, with a sob, she returns Sophie's embrace.

I go to join them but then hear a tinny voice coming from the scrubbing brush. "Hello? Hello?"

Copying how Paula had used it I gingerly pick up the brush and speak into it. "False alarm."

Dropping the brush to the floor I turn back to Paula and Sophie.

They stare at me. Stare at the hand with which I'd saved Sophie's life.

*

I sit, the mug of hot chocolate in front of me gradually going cold.

Upstairs Paula is putting Sophie to bed. After she had stopped crying Sophie had drunk her hot chocolate, it was supposed to calm her nerves but her hands trembled as she gripped the mug. She was scared. Not just because she had nearly died. She was scared of *me*.

Even as Paula carried her upstairs Sophie had stared at me, afraid that I might still carry out my threat to hammer the glass through her neck. And that this time I might not save her.

I study my hands, slowly turning them over to examine both front and back. They look the same as they always have. The tiny hairs that run along my skin, the white scars on my fingers where my grip slipped whilst working on car repairs. Nothing has changed.

But now my hands can give Paula orgasms, heal her migraine, and bring Sophie back from the brink of death.

What other miracles can I perform?

Slowly I raise my hands to my head. The Pick's doesn't bother me personally but without it Sophie would never have been injured. And even though I somehow managed to save her I can't stand the way she looked at me as Paula carried her upstairs.

Let's see just how powerful these healing powers are.

Cupping my hands over my head I press down, flattening my hair against my skull. I squeeze my eyes shut and concentrate.

I hold the pose for five seconds.

Ten seconds.

Thirty seconds.

How long will it take to work?

After a minute and a half I open my eyes. I don't feel any different. But then, I never felt any different while the disease destroyed my personality so I shouldn't feel any different with the disease gone, my personality restored.

So how can I tell if it worked?

A harsh ringing erupts through the lounge. I jump up, startled. Then I breathe again; the sound is familiar, it's coming from the tray thing Paula used to call the ambulance.

Good. If I can remember how to use this it proves the Pick's is gone.

I stand in front of the tray, helpless.

Fuck.

The ringing persists. Frustrated, I smash the tray to the floor. The brush thing on top of it flies loose.

"Craig?" says a small, distorted voice. "Is that you?"

Cautiously I go down on all fours and put my head up to the brush. "Hello?"

"Craig, it's Zoë. I've got some news for you."

"Not now, Zoë."

"God, this is a bad connection. Sounds like you're about a foot away from the receiver. Anyway, what I've got to tell you –"

"I said, not now."

A pause. It's hard to tell past the faint background crackle but when Zoë speaks again her voice sounds brittle. "Are you avoiding me because we slept together?"

I don't have time for this. I'm not sure how to get the tray to break the connection so I just pick it up and hurl it against the wall. That seems to work.

As I dump myself onto the sofa footsteps sound on the stairs behind me. Turning, I see Paula standing on the bottom step, her fingers toying nervously with the cross about her neck.

"Sophie's too scared to sleep alone so I've said she can sleep in our bed." Paula hesitates, then tells me the rest. "But she doesn't want you to sleep with us."

My Adam's apple works up and down a couple of times as she waits for an answer.

"Okay."

"I'll –" She brushes a lock of loose hair from her face. "I'll get you some blankets."

She turns to go. I call out to her.

"I was bluffing about shoving the glass through Sophie's neck."

"I know."

She walks back up the stairs.

I sit on the sofa, frightened and alone. The lounge feels as big and empty as a tomb.

*

Breakfast passes in silence. Paula and Sophie sit in the kitchen eating cereal. I sit in the lounge, the blankets of my makeshift bed rucked up around me, and eat a bowl of leftover chilli con carne. No one mentions what happened last night. The only sound is the scraping of spoons against bowls.

I tried to cure the Pick's again after Paula left me the blankets. Still no luck.

I think back to the shard of glass protruding from Sophie's throat, the blood trickling from the wound, the horror in her eyes. The memory terrifies me but something else scares me even more.

As the Pick's progresses my attitudes and behaviour will change more and more. Eventually I'll reach the point where if Sophie get injured again I won't care.

I look over at her. She sees me and turns away, dropping her gaze to her cereal.

I put the bowl of chilli on the table. I've lost my appetite.

The doorbell rings.

Paula moves to open it but I jump up from the sofa and beat her to it. I need something to distract me. Something trivial, something crushingly and mindnumbingly dull.

I open the door to find two policemen standing on the doorstep.

"Mr Warner?"

I give an exasperated sigh. "Look, that call for the ambulance last night wasn't a hoax, it was an honest mistake. We really thought we needed it when we called."

The policemen look confused. "I don't know anything about any ambulance," says the older, more grizzled of the two. "We're here about Zoë Wilson."

I try to think why Zoë might be in trouble. She occasionally messed around with drugs – cannabis, ecstasy – but nothing too heavy. Certainly not anything serious enough to involve the police.

"I'm afraid we've got bad news." The policeman's heavily-lined features radiate sympathy. "She died last night."

*

I hate funerals.

Or maybe I used to like them, I don't know. But this one I hate.

Zoë shouldn't be dead. She should be laughing and joking and making love with a wild, uninhibited passion.

But she lies still and motionless in a wooden box and we sit in our pews, listening to the vicar read out the eulogy.

Zoë was never religious, her recent interest in New Age spirituality notwithstanding, but the vicar at the crematorium explained that a token amount of Christianity had to be included in the service, so we had some hymns and prayers. I think Paula would have liked more of them but she didn't arrange the funeral, Zoë's parents did.

They sit beside us in the front row of the crematorium. Her father, his suit black and his face grey, his quiet stoicism betrayed by the bleakness of his gaze. And her mother, crumpled by grief, a handkerchief to her wet eyes, her lip trembling as she strives to contain her emotions just long enough to make it to the end of the service, to complete this last goodbye to her daughter. Her husband's hand strokes her back mechanically, trying to offer solace even though he has none of his own.

I'd visited Zoë in the chapel of rest. Lying in her coffin, her face waxen, unreal, as though she'd been replaced by a model from Madam Tussaudes. After I'd been left alone with her I pressed my hands to her head and willed her to live.

Nothing.

Considering the embalming fluid in her body and the stitches in her eyes it may not have been such a bad thing that I couldn't revive her. Still, at the time I stormed out of the funeral parlour in a cold rage, furious that my newfound healing powers had failed me.

Maybe if I'd seen her as soon as she died I could've revived her. But the police didn't let me see the body, they had Zoë's parents for an ID. They only wanted to talk to me because I was the last person to speak to her before she died.

She'd been drinking. And then she snorted some ketamine. The drug didn't mix well with the booze. The police found her lying in a pool of her own vomit, surrounded by printouts from the research she'd been doing for me. Photos of my mandala and the mad guru's visions of God.

Stupid way to die.

The police treated it as a suicide, Zoë knew better than to drink while taking 'Special K', although they did briefly toy with the idea of foul play. One constable, who'd obviously watched too many TV detective shows, thought maybe the call for an ambulance was an attempt to establish an alibi. But then it turned out Zoë had actually died several hours later. There was still a slight worry about my Pick's disease – who knew what I was capable of with my ever-changing moral landscape? Paula scotched that idea by explaining that she'd locked all the doors to the house and kept the keys on her in case I wandered off during the night. That surprised me, I thought all the Chubb keys were hanging up on their respective hooks the way they always did at night. I need to pay attention to what changes Paula is making around me.

And our locks weren't the only problem. Zoë's flat was locked from the inside.

The vicar's eulogy ends. She looks out upon the mourners. "Would anyone else like to share their memories of Zoë?"

I stand. Paula tugs at my sleeve, nods furiously at Zoë's parents. Ignoring her I stride up to the pulpit.

Facing the mourners I see Paula close her eyes in despair. She thinks I'm going to make a scene. Maybe I am. I don't know if what I'm going to say is appropriate but I have to say it.

I clear my throat. "Zoë and I were lovers. And for a long time after that we were friends. I'm going to miss her."

There isn't really anything left to say after that so I walk back to my seat. A couple of people nod their heads approvingly. I expect Paula to be happy, or at least relieved, but as I sit she shoots me a resentful glare.

*

"But her parents have invited us back to the wake."

"I know, but I've got a splitting migraine."

I frown. "Yeah, you've got a migraine but Zoë's dead. Which do you think is worse?"

"That's typical. You always thought more of Zoë than you did your own family. You even managed to control your disease today, stopped yourself making a scene. You never do that for us."

"No. All I did was save Sophie's life after you almost killed her."

Paula flinches, as though I've slapped her across the face.

I glance over to where the other mourners mill about in front of the plaque that's been put up for Zoë. Wreathes lay upon the ground. I catch a glimpse of Justin walking to his car. Another reason I want to go to the wake. I need to talk to him about his guru.

He looks dazed as he climbs into his car; numb. He doesn't even look in my direction.

I turn back to Paula. "Just five minutes, okay?"

She puts a hand to her head. "This migraine is killing me. Let's just make our apologies and go home."

"For fuck's sake!" I clamp my hands on her head and perform another improvised Indian Head Massage. Maybe I can't cure my Pick's disease or raise the dead but I'm sure I can sort out a bloody migraine.

Paula screams, twisting in agony at my touch. I jump back and she falls to the ground, sobbing. I stand over her, staring at my healing hands that can suddenly only unleash pain.

*

Opening my email takes a good ten minutes.

The various contraptions in front of me have coloured stickers corresponding to Paula's notes telling me how to work the bloody things. The icons are listed there too. It's remembering to move the bar of soap with the wire dangling from it to the correct icon that's the problem. There's a note in huge block capitals telling me to move the bar of soap across the desk so that it moves the little arrow onto the icons and *not* to press the soap directly onto the icons on the screen.

Eventually, tired and pissed off, I find my messages.

Normally Paula would do this for me but she's been avoiding me after what happened at the funeral. She leaves readymade Mexican meals in the freezer, attaching a little note to the microwave in case I forget how to use it. Sophie sleeps with Paula and I'm relegated to Sophie's room, my feet hanging over the end of her bed. My dirty clothes vanish and then reappear in Sophie's room the next day, washed and ironed. Neither Paula nor Sophie talk me to me if they can help it, leaving the room as soon as I enter.

Three days it's been now. Frustrated by lack of company I've tried using that tray thing to talk to people but even on the occasions when following the notes actually lets me get through most people are at work when I try to speak to them. Afternoon TV just brings old films and a discussion show on adultery. So I've turned to the email.

There's only one new message.

It's from Zoë.

Of course. She's the only person who knew that I was thinking of attempting to use email again.

The message is dated as an hour before she died. The subject heading is 'God Info'.

```
Craig,

    I hope you had a good reason for hanging up
    on me.   If you're just being an arsehole
    then you don't deserve me emailing this to
    you.

    Please don't be an arsehole.

    Zoë
    XX
```

God Info.doc 58802 bytes

I wonder what I would've done about Zoë if she hadn't died. Left Paula for her? Kept her as a bit on a side? Forgotten the whole thing? Or, as the Pick's disease worked its way through my brain, all of the above?

I don't know. And I don't feel any guilt over this, even though the discussion show I watched earlier suggested that adulterers should feel guilty. I'm just sorry that she's dead.

It takes me five minutes to work out that I need to move the arrow over the underlined text if I want to read what Zoë has sent me.

Text and graphics spring onto the screen. It's a list of articles about Justin's old guru and his descent into madness.

I start reading.

Visions of the Lord

```
Michael   Stevenson's   devotion   to   spiritual
matters    initially    appeared    to   be    his
```

41

salvation.   Instead it proved to be his
damnation.

Stevenson, a recovering alcoholic, first
turned to yoga to ease his chronic back pain.
But the more spiritual side of the discipline
proved to hold an unexpected appeal to him,
becoming far more fulfilling than any bottle
of booze could ever hope to be.

He researched other forms of meditation,
creating his own spiritual regime, and began
teaching it to his students.   Displaying a
hitherto untapped grasp of business he soon
had a chain of schools.   Financial security,
inner peace; it looked like he had it all.

Then he saw God.

The vision drove him mad.   Some people say he
had been experimenting with ketamine to aid
his meditation, others say it was a genuine
vision of God.   Either way he became a
recluse in his plush Sussex mansion, attended
to by private psychiatric consultants.   His
visions grew steadily worse.   He claimed that
his followers were demons, out to destroy his
work.   Legend has it that he escaped from his
mansion and when his warders returned him to
his room he was covered in blood.   And it
wasn't his own.

But Stevenson returned to the mansion covered
not just in blood but in bruises, and one of
his testicles had been crushed.   A few months
later he took his own life, hanging himself
from his bedroom ceiling.

Perhaps now, in Heaven, he has seen God again
and finally knows peace.

The other articles say pretty much the same thing. But they don't
interest me as much as the accompanying pictures.

There are several artist's impressions of Stevenson's various visions of God. No two look the same but they still look horribly familiar. One is a face made up of dead and dying bodies. Another face shines with dreadful beauty. Another is a collection of dying stars and galaxies.

Stevenson's visions of God are the same as mine.

Elated, I punch the air. Here's the proof that I'm not just hallucinating! But then I consider how Stevenson ended up and my joy shrivels.

And when I see the other pictures my joy not only shrivels but dies.

Photos of Stevenson, taken a few months before he died. His grey hair stands on end and his manic gaze blazes from his emaciated face. Behind him stand a group of his followers, looking uneasy at their guru's fall from grace. One of them is Justin. He's wearing a T-shirt and his wiry arms are not yet decorated with tattoos.

And another photo. This one taken at Stevenson's funeral. Justin is there again, dressed all in black. On the back of his hands can now be seen the black ink of his tattoos, reaching across his flesh, almost as if attempting to turn him into a living shadow.

I chew on my thumbnail. Justin got his tattoos to cover his stab wounds... He got his stab wounds a few months before Stevenson died... Stevenson was brought back covered in blood and bruises... Justin would've got out of hospital around the time of Stevenson's death...

I think of the steel shutters that dropped down behind Justin's eyes when he thought he might have to fight me. The way his ethics disappeared at the prospect of violence. He would've done whatever it took to stop me.

And right then I know. I know that Justin killed Stevenson. Lying in hospital for months, seething over Stevenson's betrayal, waiting for a chance to get his revenge. Getting in to see Stevenson would've been easy. He faked the suicide, waited for someone to find the body, and then acted the shocked disciple.

And then it hit me. If he's faked a murder to look like suicide once maybe he's done it twice.

He knew he'd blown things with Zoë. Maybe he'd even found out about her sleeping with me. So he killed her. Got her so drunk she didn't know what she was doing then got her to snort the ketamine.

Bastard. Evil fucking bastard.

I jump up from the computer and run from the room.

He won't get away with it.

*

My car mounts the pavement, swerves, then drops off the kerb back onto the road. I bring it screeching to a halt, the smell of burning rubber filling my nostrils. I don't know why Paula says I'm a bad driver. Wish I could've figured out what that crunching noise was every time I changed gear though.

Jumping out of the car I run towards Justin's flat. Beneath my feet the car's tracks arc across the road like angry serpents.

Paula doesn't know I'm here. She's picking up Sophie from school. Locked all the doors to stop me wandering. I found the keys easy enough though, she might as well not bothered hiding them, it was like I already knew where they were. My brain may not work the way it used to but Paula's still does. I knew she'd hide the keys in the coffee jar. Same place as my car keys.

As I run up to Justin's front door the metal rod I took from my toolbox hangs heavily in my coat pocket, weighing the material down so the coat doesn't sit straight on my shoulders. With each step my leg bumps up against the solid metal.

I'll need it to take that psycho down.

I stab at his doorbell. The chime is deep, melodic, like a Buddhist monk humming for Enlightenment. It doesn't do anything to calm me.

Justin doesn't answer the door. I ring again.

Still no answer.

Right. Drawing the rod from my pocket I pull it back to smash through the window situated at the top of his door. As I pull back my right hand my left brushes against the door and the door swings gently open.

I barge through the door, into the lounge. No one there. On into the kitchen. Empty. Fling the bathroom door open. Nothing. Only place left is the bedroom.

Locked.

The doorknob rattles in my hand. I kick at the door, the shock of the impact running up my leg. The door flexes in the doorframe but doesn't open.

"Justin!" I scream. "Open up, you bastard!"

I kick again. An angry crack, like the snapping of a thick branch, and the door flies open.

Barging into the room I brandish my rod. But then I see what's inside the room and I stop dead.

Justin stares up at me, a snivelling heap of naked flesh, covered in blood. Light flickers off the blade in his hand as he continues carving up his own body. On the floor in front of him lie photos of Stevenson's visions of God and a copy of my personal mandala.

"I've seen God," he whimpers. "I've seen God."

Over and over again.

*

I toss my mandala onto my garage workbench. The garage door bangs shut behind me. Grabbing my portfolio of paintings my fingers scramble madly as I tear it open.

I don't have long. Paula and Sophie will be home soon.

Pulling out my paintings of God I lay them side by side, mimicking the collage that Justin had created. The images overlap, creating a new picture, a jumble of shapes and colours that make no sense yet somehow has a strange unexplainable order to it. Finally, satisfied, I place my mandala at the centre of the collage.

I breathe, slowly, forcing my panicked gasps into the soothing rhythm of pranayama. I stare at the paintings and the mandala. Maybe this isn't such a good idea.

Whatever Justin saw it only became clear to him after meditating on my mandala. If I try the same meditation I might end up as mad as him. Sitting gibbering, drawing a knife across his flesh, the bright red of his blood obscuring the black of his tattoos. Terror in his eyes, tears mixing with the saliva dribbling from his slavering jaws. In his left hand he grasped his penis, the soft flesh torn by the knife blade, the glans not quite severed, just hanging limply from its new fleshy hinge.

I don't want to end up like that.

So crazy that he barely even registered my presence. Just kept whittling away at himself. If he kept it up sooner or later he'd slice an artery.

Good.

Keeping out of range of the knife I tried to get a better look at the mandala he'd been using. It was definitely the same design as the one he had given me. A couple of pieces of foil lay next to the mandala, a white powder upon them. Ketamine. And one of his Jung textbooks, lying open, a line of text highlighted in yellow – 'Enlightenment is not imagining figures of light but making the darkness conscious.'

He'd finally got to see God. And it had driven him mad.

But I didn't understand why seeing God had driven Justin, and before him, Michael Stevenson to commit murder. I hadn't developed any sudden psychotic urges. Was it because I hadn't used ketamine?

I needed to know. But I couldn't stay there. I wouldn't be able to concentrate on my meditation in the midst of all this chaos. Besides, Justin might decide to attack me whilst I was in my trance.

Snatching up his ketamine I ran to my car and raced home.

Now I sit cross-legged on the cold garage floor, a line of ketamine on my toolbox, a tube of paper in my hand.

I gaze at the mandala as it sits atop my pictures of God. Doing this will either answer all my questions or else drive me irretrievably insane.

I snort the ketamine.

*

"Art is a lie that makes us realise truth."
Pablo Picasso

Reality warps around me.

Time and space turn to a viscous liquid, supporting my body with a strange languid buoyancy. Stars and planets dance around me, one second dwarfing me and the next becoming so tiny that I could contain them all in a single pore of my skin. The colours of the planets flicker, changing from red to blue to yellow to green, working their way across the palette. And the stars shine so brightly, like diamonds; in the past I have only seen them as cheap cut glass imitations. They wink at me, as if conspiring in some vast cosmic joke.

It's all breathtakingly beautiful. But there's no sign of God.

Well, if He won't come to me I'll just have to go to Him. Leaning forward I kick out with my legs, my arms dragging me through the strange liquid.

I swim across the universe.

There's a small cluster of stars to my left. I head towards them, for no other reason than they're the objects that are closest to me. But then reality twists round on itself like its taken up yoga and suddenly the stars are out of my reach, hiding in a distant corner of infinity.

This isn't right. I should've seen God by now. Something's wrong.

Slowly I get the sense of something behind me, watching. I turn but time slows and space stretches, it takes an hour to move a millimetre and I have to turn halfway across a universe.

Finally, *finally*, I complete my turn and see what stands behind me. My eyes go wide and my mouth drops open.

Universes piled upon universes; the laws of physics altering, splintering, dissolving into absurdity: a labyrinthine network of other dimensions, the different realities viewed through portals like cosmic peepholes – portals leading to Earth, or a universe of pure intellect, or a universe of pure love. And one which leads only to infinite blackness.

And behind it all, connecting the whole thing together, stands God.

But this isn't God as I've seen Him before. Without the filters of petty religion to filter Him, diluting His essence, He burns with a fierce purity that dwarfs everything, even the multiverse that He's created.

I stare at Him. It's wrong to refer God as male – God has no gender and God is all genders – but I can't think of any other term by which to describe Him.

God's beauty is so great it nearly reduces me to tears of joy. As I gape at Him waves of love and compassion and tenderness roll towards me. My hands start to tingle, as I look down at them they begin to glow. I realise this is where my healing powers come from. I'm blessed with the tiniest fraction of God's splendour. And yet God contains so much more than joy.

This new sensation is, I realise, the sum of God's feelings towards humanity.

The emotion hits me and my face falls.

Total indifference.

Bewildered, I search for some sign that God cares for humanity, that we are His chosen ones.

Nothing.

God doesn't even know we exist. We're so insignificant that we don't even rate the tiniest flicker of His awareness. We're an aberration, a tiny piece of feedback that sparked into life when two other pieces of reality momentarily clashed together.

And then, as I probe God's vast being, I realise that things are so much worse than that.

God doesn't know we exist because we live in a blind spot on His brain. A blind spot caused by our very existence. Humanity, the freak birth, the cosmic accident, is a tumour on God's brain, slowly driving Him insane.

We're killing God.

⁂

I hang in space, unable to take in the enormity of my discovery.

As I stare at God, aghast, a tiny dark arrow flickers across Him. In my head it would be the tiny electric spark of a neurone but on God it becomes a jagged black shadow, sweeping across the cosmos. It's joined by another, and another. Soon a huge cloud of the shadows swarms about Him.

As their swirling continues God trembles. A terrible wrath grows within Him and one of the realities within the multiverse blinks out of existence.

I gasp. Who knows how many life forms had lived in that universe? How many families, how many civilisations. And now they're gone.

The terrible thing is that I sense God doesn't know why He destroyed that universe. He just lashed out in His madness. Unthinking, uncaring.

This can't be happening. God does care for us. He *does*.

Tears streaming down my face I throw back my head and scream at Him. "Care for us, you fucker!"

One of the shadows detaches itself from the others and darts towards me. Thoughts bleed from the shadow's mind and I see what it is capable of.

It and its fellows fuel God's anger, driving Him to flare into sudden rages when He should be composed purely of love and compassion. But what the shadows really want is to return home to the humanity that spawned them. Except that after touching God they are too powerful; any contact fills humans with despair, driving them insane.

Images of the shadows' work assail me. Michael Stevenson attacking Justin when Justin tried to stop him committing suicide, Stevenson finally ending his torment months later with a hangman's noose. Zoë, her mind shattered, weeping alone in her flat as she guzzles booze and snorts ketamine. Justin, not the murderer I'd suspected, merely a friend trying to fathom what had driven Zoë and Stevenson to madness but succumbing to that same madness himself, carving his flesh with his blade.

All of them preferring to die rather than endure the shadows' corrupting touch. So the shadows lurk on the spiritual plane searching for new victims, new prey.

Me.

The shadow latches onto me, its ethereal talons lancing into my brain, burning like liquid nitrogen. I reel backwards, clutching at my head, my thoughts scrambling against my skull, trying to escape the shadow's foul touch. It refuses to let me go, its grip growing ever tighter upon me.

It rapes my mind.

Memories churn, emotions and sensations blazing through me, crashing into each other as the shadow twists them, mangles them. Zoë's suicide, Paula screaming at me, Sophie with a jagged shard of glass jutting from her throat, finding out that God doesn't even know humanity exists: the shadow moulds them altogether into one huge monument to pain and despair.

My scream echoes across the multiverse.

Just when I think that I can't take anymore the shadow falls away from me. I double over, clutching my stomach. I feel like I'm going to vomit.

The shadow moves to attack me once more but then draws back just before it touches me. It skitters about before me, just out of reach, seething with frustration

I don't understand. The shadow might be only the tiniest speck of God's madness, to God it probably seems smaller than an atom would to me, but it should still surely be able to destroy my sanity as easily as it had Zoë's, Justin's, and Stevenson's.

Unless the Pick's disease is somehow protecting me. With my brain altering, my personality changing, perhaps the shadow can't grasp my mind tightly enough to rip my sanity from me as it did with the others. It can't gain a foothold on the ever-changing landscape of my dying brain.

Or perhaps it's because I'm touched by God. The Pick's allowed me to gain some of God's power, just enough to protect me from a lone shadow. But I don't just have God's love, I also have His wrath, the pain that His madness can inflict.

And I can't control it any more than He can.

The shadow continues to circle me, searching for an opening, hoping that I might still have an area of vulnerability. I back away. This creature, this wraith, may be humanity's offspring but I don't want anything to do with it.

The shadow follows me, matching my pace. Then suddenly its head whips round to look back at the multiverse. Following its gaze I see into the intricate lattice of wormholes and interdimensional portals. One of them leaps into focus, zooming in on the figures that dwell within. Paula and Sophie.

The shadow darts towards the portal. The shadow's thoughts bleed from its foul mind, trailing behind it like an oil slick of sadism and malevolence. It may not be able to take over my mind but my physical body is still back in the real world. It can use that as a gateway from which to leap to Paula and Sophie, attacking their souls, destroying their psyches.

Frantic, I chase after the shadow.

Paula's key is in the front door, scratching at the lock's tumblers.

"No!" I scream. "Go back!"

She doesn't hear me. She *can't* hear me.

The shadow dives into the portal and its body elongates, turning to a stream of blackness, stretching down, down, down to my body below.

Paula and Sophie enter the lounge. Sophie looks up at Paula, her young face filled with discomfort. "Where's Daddy?"

I'm only halfway across the array of interdimensional doorways, just level with the one filled with infinite blackness. Ahead of me the shadow's claws reach for my physical body, edging closer, ever nearer.

Holding Sophie's hand Paula wanders over to the garage. "Craig? Are you in there? Why is your car outside?"

Moving through the strange liquid that time and space have become is like trying to swim through jelly. I stare helplessly at the portal, still just beyond my reach. I'm not going to make it.

Paula pushes open the door to the garage and halts in astonishment as she sees the shadow hovering above my head. The shadow's claws touch my skull and slowly it begins to flow into my head. From outside the portal I see the whites of my eyes turn pitch black.

Sophie screams.

No, damn it! I won't let this happen!

The shadow's legs still hang outside the portal and I grab them, try to yank the creature back, away from my family. Pain flares at the shadow's touch and it twists and writhes so hard that I nearly lose my grip. But I manage to hold on and, kicking hard with my legs, I begin to swim slowly away from the portal.

Down in the physical world I see Paula push Sophie behind her. The shadow still hasn't let go of my body, the blackness hasn't left my eyes. I see the shadow use my hand to reach out to Paula. "Help me." The shadow makes my voice sound hoarse, grating. "Save me."

Paula takes the crucifix from around her neck and thrusts it towards me, holding the tiny gold cross at arm's length. "Our Father, who art in Heaven…"

I pull again and the shadow comes with me, wrenching free of my body. I keep kicking my legs, every second of contact with the shadow sending blinding pain lacerating through my brain. But still I hold on and edge closer to my goal. The portal filled with blackness.

Reaching the lip of the portal I push the shadow in. It teeters on the edge, arms flailing, its talons trying to tear at my face. And then it falls. Down it tumbles into the blackness, its own black shape now appearing almost white in contrast to the ultimate darkness in which it now finds itself. Until finally it dwindles from sight, gone.

Exhausted, I look back to the other portal. My physical body has collapsed, the shadow gone. Paula and Sophie kneel by my side, trying to revive me.

I don't have the energy to swim back over. Crossing the universe yet again would push my already shattered mental energy to its limits, it might even kill me. But I've completed my business on the spiritual plane, there's no need for me to stay here any longer.

I take one last look at an oblivious God. His immensity is incredible. No wonder He doesn't even notice us. I wonder how long it will be before humanity's presence finally kills Him.

Crying, I turn my back on Him and will myself to wake from my trance.

The garage floor is even colder than when I left. Paula's hands grip my shoulders, shaking me. When I wake a giant sob of joy nearly chokes her and she hugs me fiercely. She still has the crucifix clutched tightly in her fist.

Looking up I see Sophie standing away from me, fear and distrust etched onto her face.

Paula waves her over. "It's all right, Sophie. It's all right. God drove the demon out."

Sophie walks over, taking small, uncertain steps. When she's within arm's reach Paula grabs her, pulling her into the hug with which she is already embracing me.

"Everything's all right now," repeats Paula. "We can handle anything. Demons. Your daddy's disease. *Anything*." Tears shine in her eyes. "God is watching over us."

She looks so happy I don't have the heart to tell her the truth.

The Death of Innocence

Three weeks since the attack and I'm still too scared to leave the house.

I never found out who my attackers were or why they chose me. They insulted and threatened me before they got physical but it was all generic stuff. "What you looking at?" "You got a fucking problem?" None of it was about me. I just happened to be the first person they ran into.

Nothing personal.

They ruined my life for nothing.

*

"I'm off now, love," says Jenny, slinging her bag over her shoulder and snatching a piece of toast from my plate. Her usual last minute dash for work, interrupted for a week while she nursed me but now resumed.

"Okay," I reply. I expect my voice to be shrill, full of fear at being left alone. Instead it is dull, lifeless.

Jenny lets the toast dangle from her mouth as she jangles the car keys in her hand. Her eyes sweep the kitchen, checking she hasn't left anything behind. Deciding that she hasn't she takes the toast from her mouth and kisses Susie on the cheek. Our daughter ignores her, just continues flicking spoonfuls of baby food onto the floor. "Now you be a good girl," Jenny baby-talks. "Don't work Daddy too hard and if you really *have* to fill your nappy try not to make it the green doo-doo because you know how squeamish he is."

Jenny turns to me and her tone changes from gooey to caring. "You sure you'll be okay? I don't have to go in today, I'm owed some holidays."

"No, it's all right." I realise I'm rubbing the cast on my broken arm and force myself to stop. "I'll be fine."

"Great." She smiles and kisses me gently on the lips. The bruises are healing but they're still a little tender. "I love you."

"Love you too," I reply.

"You'd better."

We walk to the front door and kiss again. "I'll see you tonight," says Jenny and then she's gone.

I lock the door behind her.

*

Susie likes *Postman Pat*. I used to like stuff like *The Crow* and *The Long Kiss Goodnight* but since the attack I have trouble watching violence no matter how stylishly realised. Unpleasant memories begin to stir, fear starts bubbling within my chest. I know that I'm only watching a film but there's something within me that refuses to acknowledge this and my breath quickens and I start to sweat.

So now I try to lose myself in the banality of *Postman Pat* videos. Susie sits on the floor, staring at the screen, entranced by the magical figures on the TV. I wish I had that innocence again.

At least Susie is comfortable in my presence now. When I first got out of hospital I had terrified her. She twisted in Jenny's arms, trying to avoid looking at me, scared of this strange creature with the bruised, swollen face and broken teeth. When I picked her up she cried until I handed her back to Jenny. My own daughter had been so frightened of me that I couldn't even hold her.

I wanted to kill the men who had done this to me.

But I knew that if I ever found them I would be too scared to do anything. Crippled with the fear they had beaten into me. They had shown me truths about myself I never thought I would have to face. I was a coward. I didn't even fight back. Just curled up in a ball and let them beat me. I even pissed myself, the warm liquid scaring me even more – I thought it was blood – before I realised what it was. My attackers laughed themselves silly as the puddle spread across the pavement, stripping away the last remains of my dignity. They thought it was hilarious. Except for the one who didn't step back quickly enough and got piss all over his boots.

"You cunt!" he yelled. "You fucking bastard!"

He stomped on me even harder then. That's when my arm got broken. I was covering my head, trying to protect it from his kicks, and the forearm just snapped. Popped like a wishbone. I knew what my wish was, that none of this had happened, that it was all some terrible dream.

Angrily I realise I've been thinking about the attack again when I'd promised myself I wouldn't. The memories haunt me, stalking my subconscious, ready to jump out and make me remember when I least expect it. Several times I've woken in the night – sobbing – and Jenny has cradled me in her arms, whispering gentle words of comfort. She's so strong. And I'm so weak.

Postman Pat finishes. Susie looks at me. "Pa'," she says; as close to Pat as she can manage at the moment.

"Yeah, it's rewinding, sweetheart."

She crawls over to me. "Pa'. Pa'."

"Pat," I correct, lifting her onto the sofa. "Say Pat."

"Pa'."

As the tape whirrs back to the start I hear sounds outside the front door. Bottles clinking together, footsteps.

My heart jumps. I know it's the milkman but just before I was attacked I heard the clinking of bottles. Beer bottles the thugs had been carrying. One of which was used to club me over the head. The bottle felt solid as a crowbar, leaving a lump the size of a golf ball. The doctor said I was lucky the bottle hadn't shattered otherwise my face would have been cut to shreds. More ways to frighten Susie.

Outside I hear the footsteps retreating but still I wait, straining my ears for any other sounds. Birdsong, traffic -- that's a milk-float I hear, surely? – an aeroplane passing overhead, children laughing and their mothers scolding them as they move along the street; but no more movement on the doorstep.

I force myself to move. I leave Susie on the sofa – she goes back to staring at the TV screen even though it's blank. My baseball bat lies in the corner of the lounge. I pick it up.

Creeping over to the window I stare out. A beautiful sunny day; blue sky, white clouds, the streets empty apart from law-abiding citizens. Nothing wrong with this picture. Except – where's the milk-float? If it was the milkman at the door he would have a milk-float with him and there isn't one in sight.

My grip tightens around the baseball bat, the friction causing the skin to bunch up, Chinese burns on my fingers.

Maybe the milkman just parked out of sight. After all I had heard a milk-float. At least I *think* I did.

I'm just being jumpy. No one has got any reason to attack me in my own home. But no one had any reason to attack me in the street either. Maybe they've come back to finish the job. They're scared I'll identify them to the police – fat chance – or maybe they're just so bloody-minded they want to finish what they started, won't be happy until I'm dead. That article about the attack in the local paper – they could have got my address from there.

Oh God, they're back. They're going to kill me.

I turn back to Susie. She's kneeling in front of the VCR, prodding at buttons in a vain attempt to bring back *Postman Pat*. I scoop her up before she has a chance to start exploring the plug and power socket.

"Pa'," she says. "Pa'."

"Shh." Picking her up I sneak out the lounge and up the stairs.

"Pa'!" she wails. "Pa'!"

"It's all right," I whimper. "Everything's okay."

We get to her room – all cuddly toys and Teletubbies wallpaper. I shut the door then cower in the corner; Susie clasped to my chest. She struggles in my grasp. I hold her tight. She starts to cry. I put a hand over her mouth. I want to reassure her but I can't speak. I can't do anything but tremble, the tremors running through me as if my body is housing some kind of organic earthquake. The fear is out of control now; I have to surrender to it, hoping it will burn itself out.

Seconds turn to minutes, maybe even hours. There is no sound of anyone breaking in or moving through the house. Eventually I pull myself together enough to stand up. It looks as if the whole thing was a false alarm.

Still the sweat rolls off me.

I put Susie in her cot. "You be a good girl and be quiet. Daddy's got to do something." Daddy's got to find out if he's going to get the shit kicked out of him or whether he's just going mad.

I kiss Susie on the forehead and then shut her bedroom door. As I descend the stairs, the baseball bat in my good hand, I pray that if anything happens Susie will get out okay.

I go to the kitchen first. They'll try the back door. There's no broken glass – they haven't smashed the window. The door doesn't look as though it's been forced but they may have picked the lock. No – still locked.

I edge towards the front door. My knees tremble and my bladder feels like the Thames barrier. Please don't let me piss myself again.

Taking a deep breath I peep out the small window in the door, expecting to see an angry face glaring back at me. Nothing. Just the mist forming as I let out a relieved sigh onto the glass.

But they've probably done this sort of thing before, they know to keep away from the window, crouching below my line of vision.

Slowly I put the baseball bat to one side and reach for the door handle. I turn it as smoothly as possible, trying not to alert my erstwhile/would-be attackers to what I'm doing. Then I'll yank the door open, look, and slam it shut before they have a chance to react.

That's what I'm going to do.

Any second now.

My hand starts to cramp from holding onto the door handle.

Okay, it's now or never. Open the door.

I yank the door so savagely I expect the security chain to rip from the frame.

Two milk bottles sit on the front step.

Great gulps of air rack my body and my heart stops trying to smash its way through my sternum. I totally forget about closing the door and it's not until the strength goes out of my legs and I lean against it for support that it slams shut.

*

The newspaper article about the attack didn't have our address in it. I should have realised. The piece was so short it hardly had space to describe the attack let alone add any other details. It's galling to have the most harrowing experience of my life reduced to a few inconsequential lines in the local rag.

I sit in the lounge, Susie on my lap, rereading the article and a feeling of rage comes over me. My life has been all but destroyed and no one seems to care. The police promised to do everything they could to catch my attackers but they deal with dozens of cases like this, I'm nothing special.

While I was in hospital the sergeant investigating the attack came to see me for a statement. "The fingerprints from the bottles they were carrying may help with identification," he said, trying to sound as encouraging as possible. "And from the knife."

"Knife?"

"Yes, one of your assailants dropped a Stanley knife as he fled the crime scene. The two officers who came to your assistance say he was about to slice you with it when they arrived." He smiled. "Lucky escape there."

I hadn't even seen the knife, hadn't realised they were actually going to kill me. The sergeant's words of comfort left me with a bad case of the shakes.

My friends weren't much help either. They tried but none of them seemed to connect with what I was feeling. It was as if an invisible wall had been thrown up, preventing any sense of empathy. I tried talking to Chris about it when he came over one time. The first couple of visits it had just been, 'Glad to see you're okay, here's a bag of grapes' occasions. This time I tried to tell him how I actually felt.

"I don't think I'm going to be able to get over this. Emotionally, I mean."

Chris shifted uncomfortably in his chair. You had to catch him in the right mood if you were going to talk to him about emotions. "How's that then?"

"I keep thinking things would be better if I'd fought back more."

"Come off it. There's no way you can win a fight when it's four onto one. Not unless you're Bruce Lee. And even he'd probably want to bring his nunchakus along."

"Yeah, I know, but I should've *tried*. Now I'm always going to be wondering if I'm going to have the guts to stand up to anything ever again."

Chris took a swig from his beer can. "You're being too hard on yourself. Remember that time when my car got broken into, some git stole the radio? You came with me when I went to look for him. You were all right then. Give it awhile and you will be again."

"We never found that bloke though, did we? Never had to do anything about it."

"Didn't know that when we went looking. You still came."

"Chris, I was scared shitless the whole time."

He looked at me as though I had just been refused membership in some exclusive club then changed the subject; started talking about football.

Jenny wants me to see a counsellor. I told her I'm fine, that I'll be back to work any day now. She knows I'm lying. But I can't talk to a counsellor. I can't even talk to Jenny about it, not properly. If I did I'd have to tell her the truth.

Susie stirs in my lap and starts crying for food just as I decide I need to go to the toilet. I carry her through to the kitchen and put her in her highchair. I open the cupboard; Rusks – her favourite food. A bowl from another cupboard then to the fridge for milk. A spoon from the drawer and I'm ready to start mixing. "You like this, don't you?" I coo as I turn the biscuits to gooey mush.

Susie gurgles with delight and waves her arms around.

"Careful, you'll take off."

I can't hold my bladder any longer. I leave the half-prepared food on the table next to the milk bottle. Susie tries to pick up the bowl but can't quite reach. "Back in a second, sweetheart."

Into the bathroom. Fumbling with my fly. I look down and see my face reflected back at me from the water at the bottom of the toilet.

Caught off-guard I remember the attack.

The pain.

The fear.

The shame.

My secret shame, that I haven't told anyone about, that I don't even want to admit to myself.

During the attack a thought had run through my head. I don't know where it came from; some dark horrible part of myself that I normally keep locked away. But the attack unleashed it, let it run rampant.

As I was being beaten I had wished that Jenny was there. Then they wouldn't have focused on me so much; some of them would have beaten her instead. Maybe then my arm wouldn't have got broken, maybe I wouldn't have wet myself, maybe I wouldn't have been so scared.

I love Jenny, I do. With all my heart. But I still had the thought – wishing she was there to take the punishment instead of me. I didn't even care if she had Susie with her; anything so long as I was spared.

I am scum. I don't deserve to live.

My reflection stares up at me from the toilet. I piss down onto my face. After flushing I wash my hands but it only kills germs, the guilt is still there.

Slowly I walk back to the kitchen. Before I reach the door there is the crash of glass. Susie starts wailing in distress.

Oh my God! They've found me! I don't know how but they have! They're breaking in the back door!

My legs carry me to the stairs. I can lock myself in the bedroom. Susie's crying stops me. I can't leave her. I grab the baseball bat, ready to fling open the door and rescue my daughter.

I can't. I'm too scared.

Susie's crying is even louder now. She needs help.

Maybe they haven't found me. The breaking glass could have been Susie knocking the milk bottle off the table as she reached for her food. So I can calm down before going in – she's safe. Unless she cut herself on the broken glass. She could be in there bleeding to death. I need to check. But what if they *have* found me? They'll be waiting for me in there. Waiting to finish what they started.

I can't go through that again.

They won't hurt Susie. It's me they want. They're using her as bait.

Images of my attackers – stomping me with their boots, carving me with their knives – flash through my head. Next to them are pictures of Susie lying in her toppled highchair, frightened and alone, broken glass embedded in her flesh, blood pumping over the floor as her life slips away.

Oh God, I don't know what to do! *I don't know what to do!*

The door stays closed.

Susie's crying stops.

Mine starts.

Daddy's Little Girl

Daddy's going to make me a star.

He says I've got real talent and he wants to make a film with me playing the lead. I've never been in a film before.

I didn't know that Daddy knew how to make films but he says he has made some with a few of his friends. They film them with a video camera and sell them to people. I ask why I haven't seen any of these films and Daddy explains that they only made a few copies to see if people liked them.

That means there won't be any famous people in the film. I ask if Mummy will be in it and Daddy says no, it's a secret, Mummy mustn't know about it. He wants to surprise her. I clap my hands and giggle as I think of the look on Mummy's face when she sees the film.

*

Daddy buys me a new dress for the film. A nice pink one. And some ribbons for my hair. I want to know if I'm going to wear makeup but Daddy says I'm too pretty to need any. Besides, makeup is for boring old grownups, he wants me to look like the pretty young girl that I am.

I sing to him and he tells me my voice is beautiful. After that I do a little dance for him and Daddy says I look like a little ballerina.

I ask if my friends can be in the film when we make it. Daddy thinks about it and then smiles. Maybe if he and his friends make some more, he says.

*

Not telling anyone that I'm going to be in a film is hard. I'm so excited I feel like I'm going to burst. It's like someone has put a balloon inside my tummy and now they are pumping it up so that it keeps getting bigger and bigger and bigger. But I don't tell anyone, I'm a good little girl.

Daddy knows that I'm good with secrets. I never told Mummy about the time I got up in the night to go to the toilet and found Daddy watching a film. He asked me not to tell Mummy because it was a scary film and she didn't like that sort of thing. It must have been scary because when I came in Daddy jumped as if he were really frightened. But ever since then he knows that I can keep a secret.

There are times I've nearly told people about the film though. I'm dying to tell Susie and Lorraine because they're my best friends. And when Wayne Bradley teases me in the playground I want to tell him that he's just a silly little boy and that *I* am going to be a famous film star.

I nearly told Simon Jacobs once, just because I thought he'd be a good person to keep it secret; he never talks to anyone. No one likes Simon. 'Cos he's so quiet. *And* he smells of poo. At least everyone says he does. I've never been close enough to tell.

Even Simon's own daddy doesn't like him. He can't do because his daddy is one of my daddy's friends who are going to help him make the film. If Simon's daddy liked Simon he would use him in one of his films. But he can't have, otherwise Simon would be famous by now. Besides, I saw Simon crying once. Just sitting in the corner of the playground sobbing his eyes out for no reason. Who's going to make a film about a cry-baby?

*

I get Daddy to tell me what the film is going to be about. He says that I'll probably do some singing and dancing and then he and his friends will play some games with me. That doesn't sound like a very good story to me but Daddy says that's what the people who'll buy the film will want.

When I ask him what sort of people will watch it he goes quiet for a moment. Then he starts talking again, telling me that he thinks he'll be able to make money on the film. He talks about selling it all round the country and probably abroad as well. With all that money, he says, he'll be able to buy me lots of presents.

But I'm still thinking about all the different people who will watch my film. People all across the world will watch me and know my face. I'm going to be famous.

*

I'm getting really impatient to make the film. But Daddy says we can't do it unless Mummy goes out or it'll spoil the surprise. I'm fed up waiting. I want to make the film! I can tell that Daddy is tired of waiting as well. He wants to start the film as much as I do.

*

Mummy's going out tonight. There's going to be some sort of party where she works. She tells me she can't take me because it's a party for grownups. She looks surprised that I don't mind but she doesn't know about the film. Daddy says that he will stay at home to look after me as he doesn't feel very well. Mummy says okay then kisses me on the cheek and tells me not to stay up too late.

After Mummy leaves Daddy phones his friends and asks them to come round. Then he takes me into my bedroom and helps me change into my dress. He ties the ribbons in my hair then asks me to do a twirl. Daddy gives a little gasp and says I look beautiful. His voice sounds funny.

We go into the living room and Daddy pulls the curtains. I sit down and watch TV while we wait for his friends. I hope they get here soon. Making the film is going to be so much fun. And afterwards I'll be rich and famous just like Daddy promised.

Daddy's going to make me a star.

Mr Nice Guy

Alex maintained that he hadn't thought about Andrea for at least a year. He was lying of course.

He couldn't forget the night he had lost his virginity, Andrea impatiently directing his nervous fumblings. At the time he knew he loved her, now he pretended it had just been rampaging hormones. That lie – along with the way their relationship had ended – tainted the memory, turned it into a sham. Yet still he thought of her, longed for her.

So it was a shock when he heard that she had died.

*

"Why can't I get a girl?"

The question sounded more plaintive than Alex had intended, a little too whiney. But he had asked it now and he waited for Craig's answer.

His flatmate took a swig from his can of lager then glanced round their lounge, taking in the Nine Inch Nails and Marilyn Manson CDs scattered on the cupboards; the teetering pile of *Sandman* and James O'Barr graphic novels on the coffee table; the DVDs spread on the floor, mixing with the tangle of wires from the PlayStation. "Well, it can't be your housekeeping skills that's putting them off."

"No, seriously mate, I want to know." He waved his hand in drunken emphasis. "Why can't I get a girl?"

"Well, to be honest it's 'cos you're too nice."

"Eh?"

"You're Mr Nice Guy. You listen when women talk to you, you agree with what they say. When you do that women just want you for a friend. You've been like that ever since school. You're too nice for your own good."

62

Alex frowned. "I'm a Goth for fuck's sake. I worship the dark romance of nihilism. How can *I* be too nice?"

"Just because you're a drama queen doesn't stop you being nice." Craig opened another lager. "Besides, whenever you fancy a bird you always go all soppy, writing them poetry and scampering after them like a big puppy."

Alex shifted uncomfortably on the sofa. "Women *like* puppies."

"Not enough to fuck 'em."

They sat, sipping their lagers, watching *The Matrix* flicker across the TV screen. Alex was tempted to point out that Craig didn't have a girlfriend either but decided against it. Craig had been girl-shy ever since Emma had broken off their engagement. No point in reopening old wounds.

Alex reached for another can of lager but could find only empties. He climbed unsteadily to his feet. "Going to the fridge. Want anything?"

"Last night's pizza."

"Right." Alex went to the kitchen. Too nice! Him! Bollocks!

He remembered the stuff he'd got up to as a teenager. Drunkenly puking on his aunt's brand new carpet and blaming it on the dog; borrowing his dad's car and crashing it into the rear wall of the garage when he brought it back; staining the bath for weeks after dyeing his blonde hair to a more Goth-like black. And the girls – he'd played tonsil tennis with some of the best-looking totty in his year. Although admittedly he never actually got to sleep with any of them.

Until Andrea.

It felt strange to think of her in that way now she was dead; his memories of her suddenly gaining a necrophiliac twist. Andrea would probably have liked that. And she would probably have enjoyed his twinge of guilt even more.

He'd fallen in love with her the first moment he saw her. With her pale skin, long black hair, and hourglass figure she had looked like a teenaged Morticia Adams. She was the figurehead for the sixth form Goths. The real Goths, not the wannabes like him and Craig. They might have the same taste in clothes and music but Andrea always made it clear that he and Craig were geeks.

Alex knew she was right. She had a craziness that he just couldn't match. As a fourth former she'd left a steaming dog turd in the headmaster's office after he forced her to remove her heavy black eyeliner. Another time she got barred from the local pub; she snuck back in, hid in the gents and snapped a Polaroid of the unsuspecting landlord as he took a piss. The next day the landlord found posters of his flaccid cock plastered all over the outside of the pub. With a wild streak like that Alex knew that he could never do anything to get Andrea to take him seriously.

But then one night Andrea's boyfriend dumped her; in the middle of a party, in front of everybody, and she was drunk and tearful and she didn't know who to turn to.

Alex offered to take her home.

His heart pounded as she led him into her bedroom. His skin tingled, suddenly supersensitive. He didn't know what he was doing, he knew he wasn't saying the right things, he felt sure he was doing it all wrong, making a total fool of himself.

It was the best night of his life.

Of course Andrea got back together with her boyfriend the following day. Alex wandered around the sixth form block, heartbroken.

He wrote her a poem, his pain and love spilling out onto the page. Surely when she read it she would see sense and return to him.

A week later he finally worked up the nerve to shuffle up to her in the sixth form lounge and ask if she had read the poem. She laughed in his face. "Yeah, I read it. 'Oh, Andrea, I shall love you always.' Well, I don't love you. For fuck's sake, we only had one lousy shag. And I do mean lousy."

His cheeks burned.

Smiling evilly, Andrea rummaged in her pocket, pulled out a crumpled piece of paper, stained red. "Here, it was a shitty poem but it made a great sanitary towel."

She threw it at him.

The ball of paper bounced off his chest and landed at his feet. He stared at it, tears pricking at his eyes. Bad enough that she had used it as a sanitary towel... but keeping it to show him? Did she really hate him that much?

Andrea swept imperiously past him and out the lounge. Alex stood where he was, devastated, the rest of the sixth form laughing uncontrollably at his misfortune.

Then he did the one thing that he shouldn't have done. The thing that tore down the last remnants of his tattered dignity.

He picked up the poem and put it in his pocket.

Back in the here and now he cringed at the memory. Even worse, he still had the poem somewhere, packed up with all his other teenaged scribblings. Despite everything Andrea had put him through, and even though she was now a cold, hard thing buried deep beneath the ground, part of him still wanted her back.

Shit, no wonder he never had any luck with women.

*

Alex wandered through the store, scanning the DVD titles, looking for the latest *Buffy* box-set. Craig's birthday was coming up and he had a Sarah Michelle Gellar fixation.

As he eyed the shelves Alex nodded his head in time with the music blaring from the store's sound system. Goth metal. Not usually considered to be the best way of enticing customers into a chain store but he wasn't complaining.

The song vaguely reminded him of a poem he had written a few years back after one of his rare romantic relationships had broken up. He pulled the words from the corners of his memory:

Cardiac Failure

When your heart stops
Searching
For what will make it happy,
It's damaged beyond repair.
You become the King of Despair;
Crowned with gloomy regalia.
That's cardiac failure.

God, he really had been the worst poet on the face of the planet. He wanted to write great works like Poe; lyrical treatises on love, science, art and philosophy, expounding on the whole grand vista of human experience, touching the heart, mind, and soul. Instead he always ended up moaning that he didn't get laid often enough.

Finding the *Buffy* DVDs he reached for the box-set. A young woman reached for it at the same time. They both pulled back their hands, apologised for getting in each other's way, both reached for the box-set again, apologised again, laughed.

"How about if you take this one?" suggested Alex. "They've probably got some more out in the stockroom."

"Are you sure?" said the girl. She was short, the top of her head only reaching to his chest. As she spoke she came up on tiptoe in an attempt to reach his eye level. She did this with no trace of mockery or self-consciousness and the gesture endeared her to him.

"Yeah, take it. If they haven't got it here I can always get it down the street."

She smiled her thanks. Trying not to blush he returned the smile. Then he dropped his gaze shyly; the effort of maintaining eye contact with her twinkling blue eyes was too much for him.

The girl's crop-top exposed her tanned midriff and a tattoo written in Chinese calligraphy. He studied the tattoo in fascination then, realising he was staring, guiltily looked back up at her face. She was still smiling.

He felt a sudden surge of relief that his fashion sense had calmed down over the years. No more eyeliner, no more lipstick, his hair back to its natural blonde. Still dressed all in black but at least he looked halfway human.

He wanted to say something to impress her, something witty, something charming, but nothing came to mind.

"I, er…" Come on, Mr Poet; weaver of words, sultan of sonnets. Say *something*. "So, er, you like *Buffy*?"

"Yeah. But it went a bit downhill in the later episodes."

"Right. The series ran out of steam once she left high school." He shuffled his feet, trying to remind himself that he wasn't a gawky teenager anymore. "I'm Alex by the way."

"Natalie."

Okay, he'd found out her name. That was progress. Maybe this wouldn't be so bad after all. He might even manage a full conversation.

Ten minutes later he had arranged a date for that evening.

*

"You used to be in a band?"

"Not exactly." Alex paused, wondering how many credibility points he would lose for admitting the truth. "I wrote the lyrics for a band called Death of Light but that was just Craig messing about with his keyboard and me pretending to be able to sing. We never played any gigs or anything."

Natalie fiddled with her bottle of Bacardi Breezer. "You're lucky. I was forced to sing in my school play. *Guys and Dolls*. I think dogs are still howling."

Alex settled back in his seat and glanced round the pub. This was his fourth date with Natalie. The first one since they had slept together. Things were going great. He couldn't remember the last time he had been this happy.

A little stab of guilt hit him at this thought. The news Craig had given him earlier this evening should have upset him more than it had.

Craig still had a tenuous connection with Caroline Winters, one of Alex's old girlfriends – she was a friend of a friend of a friend. The news had grapevined back to Craig that Caroline had died a couple of days ago. She had been 25.

For some reason this didn't affect Alex anywhere near as much as he thought it would. Obviously he was saddened and he and Craig would

66

send a wreath to the funeral, might even attend the service itself if they felt they weren't intruding upon Caroline's family's grief. But he didn't experience the same pangs as when he heard about Andrea's death. Of course opening a newspaper to discover a story about your first love dying in a car crash was totally different to hearing of an ex-girlfriend's demise passed on as second-hand gossip but even so…

He had loved Caroline once. He should be more upset. Their break-up had been the inspiration for 'Cardiac Failure' for Christ's sake. Admittedly when he heard the news the horrible hollow feeling that always passed across his chest and gut whenever he learned of a friend or relative's death had hit him. But only briefly. He didn't shed even a single tear.

Pushing these thoughts aside he concentrated on Natalie once more. Her bubbly personality and glowing smile outshone his uneasy feelings of death and guilt. "You look great tonight."

She giggled. "I think you've mentioned that already. Five or six times."

"No, before I said you looked dazzling, beautiful, stunning, radiant, and enchanting. But I'm running out of synonyms." He toyed with his beer-mat. A sudden rush of honesty forced him out from behind his glib banter. "No, it's just that I can't believe this is happening. I'm still trying to work out what you see in me."

"Well, at first I was hoping you'd be rich but now…" Natalie shrugged. "I dunno, I just like you. You're a nice guy."

*

He could feel Natalie's energy through her hand. Even now, standing in the gallery looking at paintings, she couldn't remain completely still, swinging her hand back and forth, taking his hand with it.

At first he had thought that was why she had brought him along to this art exhibit; the pictures shared her sunny dynamism, her *joie de vivre*. But when he looked more closely the paintings shifted before his eyes, warping into something completely different.

Take this picture of a young couple walking hand in hand along a street. They were in love, happy as happy could be. But while the girl tried to walk forward towards the brighter, more modern houses the man lagged slightly behind, preferring to hang back among the older, more antiquated buildings. Pulling in different directions but unwilling to let go of each other. And then Alex realised they *couldn't* let go. They weren't just holding hands, their flesh had merged together, bone and muscle fusing, binding them with shackles made of flesh.

"Maybe we should stop holding hands," he said to Natalie. "We don't want to end up like them."

"I'll risk it if you will."

Fingers entwined, they continued making their way around the exhibit.

All the other pictures also contained ominous undertones hidden in the background. A peaceful domestic scene with smiling wife and husband, but with a jagged scar on the wife's forehead and her brain in a jar on the mantelpiece. A wife pottering happily around the kitchen whilst her husband's terrified face stared out through the window in the door of the lit oven. A wedding party with everyone cheering the bride and groom whilst the plastic bride and groom atop the wedding cake throttled the life out of each other.

Alex grinned. "This artist has even worse commitment issues than I do."

Natalie looked at him. "Why do you do that?"

"What?"

"Pretend to be all cynical when you're really a big sweetie."

He hesitated, put on the spot. "I don't know... scared of getting hurt I suppose."

Natalie nodded thoughtfully. "Been there. Not a nice place to be."

They walked on in silence for a moment.

"Don't worry," said Natalie. "*I* won't hurt you." She kissed his cheek. "Unless you cheat on me. Then I'll cut your balls off."

He laughed. He'd never been with someone who understood him so well, who knew just how to play his moods to bring him out of himself. It was like walking round on a permanent high.

The feeling had been building within him for the last few weeks without him giving voice to it. But now the limitless joy could no longer be contained. He tried to say the words earnestly, sincerely, so they would carry the weight of emotion that they warranted but his lips moved faster than his brain, blurting the words out in a sudden explosion of happiness.

"I love you."

*

He started writing poetry again.

The muse had gradually deserted him over the years, largely because adolescent angst had faded ever further into the past. But now he felt the need to compose verse, to shout his love to the world through his poetry.

"It's the most beautiful way for two people to express their love for each other," he told Craig.

Craig raised a sceptical eyebrow.

"Okay," he conceded, "it's the *second* most beautiful way for two people to express their love for each other."

He spread his old poems across the coffee table. Reading his old work helped him limber up for new poetic endeavours; it reminded him of techniques that played to his strengths, of past mistakes that he should now avoid.

"You got any of our old Death of Light songs in there?" asked Craig, looking up from his Anne Rice novel.

"Yeah, they're in here somewhere."

Craig started rummaging through the papers, flicking through exercise books, reading the backs of napkins and beer-mats. He picked up a crumpled ball of paper. "What's this one on the red paper?"

"That's the poem I gave Andrea after we broke up."

It took Craig a second to remember how Andrea had utilised the poem to help her when her period had hit but when he did he dropped it as though it was on fire. "Ugh! That's *disgusting!*"

Alex creased up on the sofa. Craig glared at him. "I can't believe you let me touch that!"

"It was worth it just to see your face!"

Craig rushed out to the bathroom, his hands held out from him as if he wished he could detach them from his wrists. "Soap! I need soap!"

Still laughing, Alex picked up the poem and smoothed out the paper. It wasn't the actual copy he had given Andrea, that was sealed up in a plastic bag for obvious hygiene reasons. This was another copy which, in a fit of Goth gloom, he had written on blood red paper.

He read the poem, his laughter fading to a chuckle and then to silence.

True Love

Why is my love unrequited
When we should be united?
I shall love you always
Until the end of days.
If another should ever steal my affection,
Poisoning my love like an infection,
Lying, making me feel blessed,
Then let my heart be torn from my breast,
Leaving me cold, unfeeling, unyielding.
Not with passion bleeding
From it as it does now,
With despair etched upon my brow.
And let the scheming harlot
Lose the scarlet

Flow that maintains her life.
An end to strife --
I will lose my loving pain
And she too will love in vein.
But, my sweet, remember this,
Even if we never steal another kiss:

I

Love

You

He sat staring at the poem for a long time after he finished reading it. Then he swallowed, trying to rid himself of the lump in his throat. Great, a god-awful poem he wrote as a teenager provoked a bigger emotional reaction than Caroline's death, even though she was one of the few women he had ever loved.

He was Mr Nice Guy all right.

*

"I'm not moving in with Natalie," he told Craig, "I'm just taking a few things over to her place. Toothbrush, razor, that sort of thing."

"You're not taking the PlayStation, are you?"

"No."

"In that case I'll help you pack."

Grinning, Alex moved round his bedroom, folding up T-shirts, selecting underwear, and putting them all in his bag. Craig leaned against the doorframe, his arms folded, watching him. "You really like her don't you?"

"Yeah." Alex smiled. "Yeah, I do."

"I'm happy for you, mate. Finding a girl who's fit and likes *Buffy*, you've hit the jackpot." Craig scratched his nose. "She hasn't got a sister has she? Or a cousin? Or even an elderly aunt; I'm not fussy."

"Sorry, mate. You're on your own."

"Story of my life."

Craig's tone was flippant but Alex still felt a twinge of sympathy for him. He patted him on the shoulder as they walked out into the lounge.

The phone rang. Alex answered it, extending the aerial. "Hello?"

"Alex? It's Hayley."

"Oh, hello." Hayley was friends with Tina, his last girlfriend. The relationship hadn't ended too badly as these things go and Alex still chatted to Tina occasionally. "How's things?"

"T-Tina's dead. She had a heart attack."

Caught off guard he floundered badly. "What? She's dead? I didn't even know she had heart problems."

"She didn't. The doctors can't explain it. It's all so –" Hayley broke off, her sobs mixing with the crackles on the line.

He waited for her to stop crying. Craig looked at him questioningly, wanting to know who had died. Cupping his hand over the receiver he mouthed "Tina". Craig's mouth fell open; Tina had been a health freak.

Hayley finally stopped crying. "I-I'm sorry. I just –"

"Don't worry. Take as long as you need."

"I just thought you should know." Hayley sniffed. "I'll make sure someone tells you the date for the funeral."

"Right. Thanks." He struggled to find some words of condolence but before he could think of anything Hayley hung up. The handset lay dead in his hand, leaving him with nothing but silence.

Folding the aerial he put the phone down.

Craig stepped over to him. "What happened?"

He told him. Craig rubbed his jaw in disbelief. "Fuck."

Alex wished he shared Craig's reaction. Intellectually he knew this was a great tragedy but emotionally it barely registered. Maybe the shock had numbed him. He hoped so.

Craig sank onto the sofa. "I can't believe that two of your ex-girlfriends have died of heart attacks within weeks of each other."

He shook his head. "Andrea died in a car crash."

"I'm talking about Caroline. That's what killed her. Cardiac arrest."

Alex stared at him, a sudden mad suspicion flowering in his mind. "You never told me that."

"I must have done."

"No," he snapped. "You bloody well didn't."

He ran into his room, yanked open the drawer in which he kept the original copy of Andrea's poem. Tearing open the plastic bag he read the smudged scrawl of his writing.

If another should ever steal my affection…
Then let my heart be torn from my breast,
Leaving me cold, unfeeling, unyielding…
And let the scheming harlot
Lose the scarlet
Flow that maintains her life.

No. This was crazy. It couldn't really happen. The deaths of his former lovers had just been coincidence. Natalie wasn't in any danger.

He decided not to take any chances. Running into the kitchen he grabbed a box of matches out a drawer and set light to the poem.

It wouldn't burn.

Flames licked at the poem but the paper refused to curl up into blackened ash. Adding lighter fluid made no difference.

Craig watched, baffled. "How are you *doing* that?"

He rushed past the bewildered Craig, back into the lounge. Snatching up the phone he speed-dialled Natalie. No answer. He tried her mobile. Switched off.

He threw the phone to Craig. "Keep ringing Natalie until you get through! If she answers tell her I'm breaking up with her! I don't love her anymore!"

Stuffing the poem into his pocket he grabbed his car keys and ran for the front door. He paused in the doorway, staring back at Craig with frantic eyes. "Remember, tell her that I don't love her!"

*

The brakes screeched as he pulled up outside Natalie's flat. Jumping out he raced for her front door.

Please let her be home. Breaking up with her was the only way to save her from Andrea's curse. Or was it his curse? He had written the poem, had wanted the pain of heartache to go away.

He stabbed at the doorbell with one hand, thumped on the door with the other.

Come on, come on! Looking round he saw Natalie's car parked down the road. If she was home why didn't she answer the door?

He thumped on the door even harder.

The door opened. Natalie peered out at him, a towel wrapped around her wet hair. "Alex, what's the matter?"

Gasping for breath, overjoyed to find her still alive, he nearly told her he loved her. But then he remembered why he was there. "I've got to tell you something."

She smiled at him nervously, not quite sure what to make of his agitation. "What? What is it?"

"Has Craig phoned you?"

"I don't know. I've been in the shower." She stepped back, opening the door wider. "You'd better come in."

They went into the lounge. The air was full of the aroma of the scented candles that Natalie loved. She sat on the sofa, unwrapping the towel and using it to dry her hair. Alex remained standing.

"So what is it you've got to tell me?"

"I –" This was the hardest thing he'd ever had to say to anyone. He loved Natalie, wanted to spend the rest of his life with her. But that's why he had to say this. Before the curse leeched his heart of all love, leaving him a cold, empty vessel. "I'm only saying this because I lo –" He broke off, clasping his hands to his head in frustration. "No, I can't tell you why I'm doing this, that'd stop it working!"

Natalie gazed at him, bemused. She was so beautiful, so trusting. If only he could find the words to tell her what he needed to say without hurting her.

"Natalie." He took a deep breath. "I –"

Natalie suddenly jerked forward, clutching at her chest, choking. She tried to stand but staggered, crashing to the floor.

"No!" He dropped to his knees beside her, cradled her head in his lap. "Don't die! You *can't* die! I'm breaking up with you! I don't love you!"

Natalie stared up at him, her eyes full of hurt at his words. Then something rattled in her throat and her body went limp.

Alex clasped her corpse to his chest. Her skin was cold and clammy but he didn't let her go. Sobs jerked his body, shaking his shoulders in time to the broken rhythm of despair.

Eventually he released her, laying her body back down on the carpet. Standing, he snatched the poem from his pocket. He tore at it furiously, tears streaming down his face. The paper remained intact. Defeated, he let the poem flutter to the floor.

His grief was a living thing, a swirling mass of woe and anguish, filling his senses, his entire being, threatening to overwhelm him. But then he felt it start to fade, ebbing gently like a receding tide. The pain left him and he knew, clearly, clinically, that it had settled in the poem he had written all those years ago.

Looking down at Natalie's corpse he felt nothing. No sorrow, no regret, nothing.

He picked up the poem, put it in his pocket and walked to the front door. If he listened carefully he could just make out the wails of torment coming from the piece of paper in his pocket.

Ignoring them he exited the flat, shutting the door behind him.

About the Author

Stuart Young has had over fifty short stories published in various magazines and anthologies including *Kimota*, *Roadworks*, *Darkness Rising*, and *The Mammoth Book of Future Cops*. His collection of short horror stories, *Spare Parts*, is available from Rainfall Books. His eBook of fantasy stories, *Shards of Dreams*, is available from Double Dragon. *Seppuka*, an action-fantasy comic set in feudal Japan, has been accepted by Engine Comics and is currently awaiting an artist.

Stuart lives in Essex, England. He spends far too much of his free time watching DVDs and reading comics.

Also Available from
www.pendragonpress.co.uk
or any bookshop by quoting the ISBN number

Nasty Snips edited by Christopher C Teague
(0 9536833 0 3; £5.99)

Shenanigans by Noel K Hannan
(0 9538598 0 0; £6.99)

Tourniquet Heart edited by Christopher C Teague
(1 8948151 0 6; £9.99 – direct price; RRP £11.99)

The Ice Maiden by Steve Lockley & Paul Lewis
(0 9538598 1 9; £4.99)

The Extremist and Other Tales of Conflict by Paul Finch
(0 9538598 2 7; £4.99)

Coming Soon

Double Negative: Book One in the Serendipity Trilogy
by Robin Gilbert

In the Rain with the Devil by Mark West

Also by Stuart Young

Shards of Dreams (*an ebook from Double Dragon*)
Spare Parts (*published by Rainfall*)